Crush

Crush

AN EROTIC NOVEL

Cécile de La Baume

TRANSLATED FROM THE FRENCH BY
RAMONA DESFLEURS

GROVE PRESS
New York

English translation copyright © 1997 Grove/Atlantic, Inc.

French copyright © 1996 Éditions Grasset & Fasquelle

Originally published in France by Éditions Grasset & Fasquelle under the title *Béguin*. The author wishes to express her special thanks to Tatiana de Rosnay.

Published simultaneously in Canada

Printed in the United States of America

FIRST EDITION

Library of Congress Cataloging-in-Publication Data

La Baume, Cécile de, 1960-

   [Béguin. English]

   Crush : an erotic novel / Cécile de la Baume ; translated from the

French by Ramona Desfleurs.

    p. cm.

   ISBN 0-8021-1620-5

   I. Desfleurs, Ramona. II. Title.

PQ2672.A162174B4413 1997

843'.914—dc21   97-21266

Design by Laura Hammond Hough

Grove Press

841 Broadway

New York, NY 10003

97 98 99 00   10 9 8 7 6 5 4 3 2 1

Crush

CHAPTER ONE

*T*he avenue at the edge of the Bois de Boulogne was deserted, dimly lit. It was the kind of place where you'd expect a proper woman to hasten her step. Amélie had just left a dinner party. She walked toward her car, keys in her hand, sensuously breathing in the fresh air. The wind rustled the leaves with the sound of crushed silk. Her pace slowed.

Her children were on vacation; Paul, her husband, at a symposium in the tropics; she was off the following day. Oh! She didn't anticipate anything extravagant or daring! She was simply enjoying letting her mind wander. All she wanted was a respite from her obligations. The extent of her daring might perhaps be limited to not going home to bed immediately.

She loved driving. She decided to drive to her parents' home two hundred kilometers away. She'd go in stealthily, surprising her children at breakfast the following morning.

1

The idea delighted her. But there was no reason to hurry. She had plenty of time. One had to admit this plan lacked boldness. Her vivid imagination covered up a lack of daring.

Making a short stop home, she got into her jeans, and a thick mottled wool sweater, then wavered in her choice of hat. On days she felt unattractive, she'd try all her hats on, one by one, looking for a shape or a shade to cap the grey silhouette she appraised severely in her closet's full-length mirror. She needed something witty for Lady Luck to be on her side, something like a boy's rakish visored cap, or a saucy beret. She'd play at being a woman of mystery in a three-cornered hat, or pose as an adventuress in a Borsalino. Nothing doing! No head cover found favor in her critical eyes. She saw herself as a ludicrous masquerader, too wan for these powerful disguises. Peeved, she slammed the closet door shut.

On up days she enjoyed game-playing, wearing a poor orphan's bonnet on a summer morning, or a coquette's veil to go to market. Some of her hats did not fulfill any of her desires, remaining where they were, condemned as a result of their failure to be nothing but samples of mistakes made by an amateur collector.

Tonight she chose a man's felt hat. She admired her reflection, bolder than usual with that hat trimmed with a black grosgrain ribbon. It gave her a smart-ass, get-a-load-of-that look. She was on her way.

She might run out of gas, but figured on getting some at Porte d'Orléans. There seemed to be some sort of commotion all around the gas station. Some kind of wrangle, she figured. She didn't care for emergencies, but there was nothing to be done. She slowed down. A young man came up to her:

—You can't drive in.

—What's up? she inquired.

—We're making a movie. We've got to reshoot this scene.

—Will it take long?

He'd turned his back on her, walking away.

Annoyed, Amélie was drumming her fingers on the wheel of her car, trying to keep cool. Silly to have a clock ticking in one's belly and be incapable of taking advantage of the unexpected she was hoping for five minutes ago. She stepped out of her car. Why not find something out about this movie?

Nothing exciting was going on. Some crew members were moving threatening poles, while others were setting up spots. The rest of the team seemed to be waiting. But where were the makeup people, and the stars she'd have found enthralling?

David had taken notice of her. He told her this much later. He gave himself the span of reshooting to find an approach. She was exactly the kind of woman he was waiting for. He observed her searching look of the scene, noted her disappointment. She was walking back to her car. He was ready to leap, but she sat patiently at the wheel. Good! There was a bit of time.

Amélie felt herself observed. She had the same feelings when she wore a hat; as if this attribute set her apart from the crowd of bareheaded women. But the looks she got were directed at her hats, she thought, so that she never bothered to check out, this night included, who might be staring.

The line of cars started moving. Amélie drove up to the pump. She had always been awkward. Glasses fell from her hand, her feet caught in the carpet, she had no sense of direction, could not read a road map. With no attendant to help her she was struggling with the cap of her gas tank, turning it the wrong way. David came close:

—Your cap? he inquired. I've got a suggestion. I'll get you out of this mess, but then you must drink with me one of the revolting cups of coffee from the machine.

—That's blackmail! she exclaimed with feigned indignation.

—Correct! David agreed ironically.

She was examining his face for disquieting signs, as though a glance could reveal a possible risk of madness or perversity. She had made up her mind to accept. He looked pleasant enough, and after all this was a public place. He couldn't strangle or rape her here.

—All right. You first! she suggested.

David turned out to be disconcertingly skillful. He unlocked the cap, filled the tank in the twinkling of an eye. All that was left for her to do was to park and join him. She searched her pocketbook for cigarettes, needing a countenance.

David came back, bearing steaming cups; tall, so dark that he appeared somber, and big, as though he had suddenly acquired substance, unless Amélie had failed to appraise him correctly a moment ago, when scrutinizing his face. Thoughtfully he held her hat while she removed her sweater, which he folded with care.

—How motherly of you! she exclaimed, masking her apprehension by the lightness of her tone.

His was polite, pleasant, a shade timid:

—That's the least I could do after being the cause of your delay. You didn't seem favorably impressed by my shoot.

—So it's your film? inquired a surprised Amélie.

—Yes, but no big deal. David was brushing this aside so as not to get bogged down in boring curriculum vitae shoptalk.

He had to mollify her, win her over. He went on:

—Let me tell you something. I'm strictly an off-key singer, but you inspire me. I'd like to serenade you.

—Right now, here? Amélie sounded disconcerted.

He started singing in a low voice, a weary smoker's growl: drinking songs, ditties from his childhood, refrains from popular tunes, an old-fashioned repertoire of Piaf, Brassens, Maurice Chevalier. Not bothering to hum discreetly, he sang at the top of his voice, unconcerned by the reaction of his team taken aback by this performance.

Amélie found it vastly amusing. She was taken off guard by his aplomb, and charmed by the ease with which he indulged in this exercise, without being in the least ridiculous. The night was taking on a surrealist coloring.

This reassuring clowning masked David's growing desire. However, he was getting restless with his mountebank act, realizing it wasn't getting him anywhere. All he knew of this woman was her first name. Alleging delicate vocal cords, he took a break. He began questioning his companion as to her status, place of birth. These narrowly targeted questions had the dispassionate quality of a poll. He was moving deliberately slowly, but Amélie remained tight as a clam. She was probing the flesh of his intentions.

He took the plunge, listing every step of his professional evolution, chronicling his love life, his marital situation. He was hoping that by opening himself wide, without cushioning the truth for the sake of decorum or personal vanity, he'd rise above the suspicion of voyeurism she might harbor when confronted by his curiosity in regard to her life. Also, he figured it would be damnably insensitive on her part to remain aloof in the face of this outpouring, indeed monstrous to avoid the obligation of reciprocity.

As for Amélie, she was trying hard to unravel the tangled skein of David's memories with their confused chronology. She was a good listener, fond of dainty romantic tidbits. Often, observing the silhouettes or faces of passing strangers glimpsed on city streets, or when she sat at one of the tables outside the cafés, she'd make up imaginary lives replete with secrets and all kinds of dramatic circumstances.

With David, however, there was no need for fantasizing. He was willing to spread his whole life before her, eager to surrender. Perhaps too much so.

At three in the morning, David relaxed, relieved to know her name and telephone number. His tone became playful. He suggested a deal. He'd narrate three of his love adventures in exchange for three of hers. She pleaded for a fair balance, since he was twenty years older. They struck a bargain: two of hers for his three. He was to begin.

At four in the morning, David inventoried the clues furnished by Amélie: married for the past ten years, residing in Paris, employed in a publishing house. Two children, no thought of divorce, and a great show of independent spirit. He was hooked, in love. He would have liked to elope with her at once; he suggested dinner the following day.

—I'm not sure I'll be back . . . , Amélie hesitated.

David stopped her:

—Listen, I'll put you at ease. I'll be at Lipp's tomorrow at nine. I'll wait, and if you can't make it, I'll have dinner by myself.

—So that's what you mean by putting me at ease! she guffawed.

His team had packed up hours ago. The cashier was dozing behind the cash register. Now that they were no longer scrutinizing one another, the place seemed deserted, strangely quiet. They went out, shivering with exhaustion.

As Amélie reached her car, she was startled by a rude shout.

—Hey, lady! bellowed the attendant, you've forgotten to pay for the gas. His dozing interrupted, he was in a vile mood.

Amélie and David exchanged amused glances, then burst out laughing. David took her arm:

—Go on. I'll take care of it. It's awfully late. If I were your husband, I wouldn't let you drive now. Be careful. Drive slowly. I don't feel like eating alone tomorrow night.

—Good night, she whispered then drove off.

—See you tomorrow! David added.

When she awoke, Amélie tried to minimize the importance of this meeting. After all, nothing forced her to have dinner with this man. By hesitating the previous evening, she had managed a way out for herself. He couldn't take offense at being stood up. Of course she had foolishly given him her address and telephone number. But were he to call, she could always send him packing. He wouldn't insist.

Having dealt with the pressure of her anxiety, she felt relieved, as when she removed from a slice of pizza the anchovies she couldn't stand. What did they have in common, after all? He was fifty, with a checkered past; she was thirty, with a clean slate. His manner was instinct and strife rather than the gentle art of conversation. As for her, she felt no inclination for power plays. When contradicted, she yielded, then regained ground by analyzing situations, turning them into anecdotes.

Glimpsing their mother's car parked in front of the stoop, Clémence and Fanny dashed up to her room, hurling themselves upon her bed. They smelled of sleep. Amélie covered their sweet, plump baby bellies with resounding kisses. Nuzzling their necks, she whispered the string of endearments that ritualized each reunion, however brief the separation. Armed with books, the girls were making sure Mother couldn't avoid the ceremony of storytelling by invoking a lapse of memory. Lying in a supine position, Amélie, each of her two daughters in the crook of an arm, began the reading while gently stroking their hair. The girls' sated bodies were sinking into well-being. However, her mind continued to wander; she had David on the brain.

She had to admit to herself he had aroused in her impulses akin to feelings of love. Upon reflection, she decided they were stronger than common character traits or affinities.

Back in Paris, Amélie was dying to keep her dinner date. However, she couldn't give in to this without setting her mind at rest about the platonic character of this adventure. She set up a fail-safe situation: She'd go, but to make sure they wouldn't sleep together, she'd have to feel unattractive. She would never give in to his desires unless she was dressed up, perfumed, ready for everything. She wouldn't dare. She delighted in her strategy, which made it a point of honor to use no makeup, select frayed underwear, and slip into an ordinary dress.

Stepping out, she assumed a resolute walk, satisfied with the informal image that confirmed her integrity. Coming close to the brasserie, her guts twisted by the concern she felt over her trivial appearance, she was sorely tempted to step into Le Drugstore's ladies' room to put on some makeup. At that very moment she saw David walking across the way, down the boulevard.

Sitting at the table, her stomach knotted, her fingers tightly gripping her knife and fork, Amélie realized her mind was a void. Generally she did not have to reach far for a subject of conversation, but she wasn't a bit hungry, not even for the steaming leg of lamb on a bed of spinach set between them.

She hated herself for her barely contained embarrassment, while David calmly conjured up all kinds of recipes in the pleasant, relaxed manner of a friend free from ulterior motives. Of course his carving the meat, feeding her like a baby bird in its nest, made her uneasy. The heavy, lustful looks directed at her by the men at the other tables accounted for her discomfort: clearly David wanted her, and everyone was privy to this secret.

Amélie had to acknowledge the obvious: Their tête-à-tête was of a libertine nature. In some fashion she bore a measure of responsibility, since both of them exuded a sexual murkiness, attracting heavy looks. She felt that their light chatter sounded fake in its disregard for their mutual attraction. She called David's attention to their gawking admirers on the one hand, and the scandalized witnesses of their provocative twosome on the other. Relaxing into the heady atmosphere, they savored the knowledge of being the main event in the restaurant's hidden nook.

David proved himself to be exquisitely thoughtful. Why not stretch our legs? he suggested after dinner. The quays along the Seine, the Tuileries gardens, rue de Rivoli . . . She allowed him to guide her through her city, arm in arm. It was like being a tourist, a stranger. Hidden within the folds of that sweet moment, her desire seemed weightless, almost effortless.

Suddenly her scruples seemed petty. It was senseless to cut the evening short. She followed David to his apartment, in one of those neighborhoods for rich foreigners, near the great hotels of the Place Vendôme, a reassuring polyglot island within a hostile Paris. The pieces of furniture were like dancers on the parquet floor due to the absence of carpets that would anchor them. Nothing untidy, no knickknacks, no travel mementos or full ashtrays. The place seemed almost uninhabited. It made her wonder whether he rented this precarious-looking space for occasional stays.

—Have you lived here long? she asked.

—About two years . . . , David answered. Since my divorce . . . I left my son with his mother in my Saint-Germain-en-Laye house so he could complete his studies before returning to Morocco . . .

Bending over her opened handbag in search of cigarettes, Amélie lent an indifferent ear to these explanations. All in all, she preferred a bohemian, marginal lover, not set in his ways, to a complacent resident of an exclusive neighborhood. David raised her face gently with his hands:

—But I didn't bring you here to bore you with my divorce case . . . , he said, eager to touch her.

Though they had met only the day before, David felt he'd been waiting for this moment for a long time. Had he heeded only his desires, he'd have taken her right there, roughly, stand-

ing up. But he mastered his impatience, tasting her, sucking
her lips, licking her face. His erection became insistent. He
almost forgot his intentions to remain civil. She was still too
serene, just slightly off-balance. He wanted to see her quiver.

—Come, he said, taking her hand.

Amélie surveyed David's bedroom with a kind of detachment that, given the circumstances, seemed almost incongru-
ous. The satin finish of the walls was anachronistic and in bad
taste, like a miniskirt worn by an aging woman. They were
white, painted in a slapdash manner disregardful of the delicately sculpted moldings. Yet despite the recent affronts to
it, the room managed to retain the opulent and comforting
atmosphere of a Haussmann-era building.

David began to undress her. Halfway stripped of all her
clothing, Amélie felt her desire and self-assurance abate. She
was in a tight spot.

By dint of his gradual, solemn plucking of her petals,
David would soon reach her old-fashioned bra, and her panties' loose elastic waist. She cringed, insecure in her body. He
was bound to be disappointed.

Distrustful and skeptical, she nevertheless noted David's
eye growing misty with wonder as he uncovered her shoulders, breasts, hips. He persisted in this miraculous absence of
any critical sense, repeating: How beautiful you are! at each
glimpse of flesh. Relieved, she stopped thinking. She was
naked, he still fully clothed. She felt she had a considerable advantage. Heedless as a schoolgirl, she leaped upon the bed and,
as at the movies, waited under the sheet's tent for the performance to begin.

Now it was David's turn to strip. He did it abruptly, as
if eager to get it over with. Big and impressive, he had kept

on his briefs. The combination of these two elements tickled Amélie's funny bone. She was convulsed with laughter, but repressed it by tightening her jaws. She needed a whiff of derision so as to mentally step away from her raw female nature, unable to produce a sentimental alibi, stirred by this body, virile to the point of caricature, and bursting with the kind of powerful sexuality that impeded sublimation, or the tempering of the crudeness of flesh.

The alchemy was undeniable. She put up the rampart of irony, keeping herself from observing David's prick for fear of growing too fascinated. But she was curious to discover the modulation of his caresses, the shape assumed by his desires, the compatibility of their senses.

He lay down next to her, taking her in his arms. Surprised by a tenderness that did not seem to go with his athletic build, Amélie felt his penis hard against her thigh.

—Do you want me to switch off the light? he inquired thoughtfully, hoping she would not insist on it.

—No, she answered.

She wanted to gauge his desire, to check it in his eyes. In the darkness he could have cheated, remained lucid while propelling her into a perilous whirlpool of emotion. Worse still, he might make violent, spiteful love that she'd mistake for passion.

—Any music? she inquired hesitatingly, inhibited by the aural precision of the sheet's rustle, the rubbing of their bodies, and the squelching noise of saliva in her mouth. David switched on his night-table radio.

She smiled, her equanimity restored. Lying on his side, David stroked her with stubby yet agile fingers. He was telling her how soft her skin was, how much he wanted to touch her buttocks, spread her thighs; crude words entangled with those of affection. Amélie moaned under the touch of these unfamiliar hands, while the swirling of her belly followed the inflections of his deep gravelly voice. He continued. He wished her warm, open, receptive of his intentions:

—Touch yourself, my love. Spread your little pussy for me. Show me how you make yourself come.

David had fantasized watching her finger-fuck herself as soon as he caught sight of her in the gas station. He had summoned in his mind the freedom of her gestures, her reserves of boldness. He envisioned becoming the prying spectator of her initiatives, the studious pupil of her amorous nature, and the consenting victim of the raptures she'd inflict on him.

Motionless and fascinated, he watched Amélie suck her middle finger with delectation, as though it had been dipped in a pot of honey, then slip it into her slit, only to offer it to him like some exotic sweet. He pulled it into his mouth, licked it, savored it, and returned it to her glistening with his saliva. He was breathing hard, his eyes dilated, his cock like the arrow of a sundial.

Amélie moistened the furrows surrounding her scarlet vulva, seeking electric sensations, her finger flat upon her clitoris. She was beginning to enjoy this exchange of voyeurism. Her legs wide open, with slow motion gestures, she turned toward David to allow him a better angle of observation.

She plunged her finger in the pearly, iridescent emulsion rising from the folds of her pussy, and breathed faster, massaging the hood on her cunt's crest.

With a greedy hand, she assaulted the delta of her cunt, moaning and moving her head in every direction, disoriented by sexual bliss like a compass in contact with a magnet. Suddenly she raised her hips, to bring her wet, dilated slit close to David's flushed face:

—Look how hot I am. Fuck me!

David made a necklace of Amélie's legs and rammed himself into her, supporting himself on his hands. He didn't want to lie down on her. He needed to see her face contract with pleasure, the blush of excitement spread upon her tits. Determined to rip open and reveal the warmth of her feelings with the tip of his rod, he plunged deep into her silky, wet, blazing depths.

—You're so juicy, my angel! I want to see you come. I'm sure you're magnificent when you come.

Amélie moaned as his dick rubbed the walls of her cunt, stifling a gasp at each of his assaults, her breathing cut short by the fireworks churning in her belly, with the violence of birth contractions.

—Say that you like it, he ordered.

Her only answer was to disgorge a cry of brutal rage as she encircled David's cock within her pulsating cunt. He smiled. It was a promising start. But if he wished to convince her of the inevitability of their union, he had to bring her to slower, more masterful orgasms. He wasn't close to being sated.

Early in the morning, a bowled-over Amélie picked up her clothes strewn on the floor. David was still asleep. She drew a hot bath in which she attempted to regain her spirits: no one had ever made love to her like this.

She had no intention to stock up her impressions without sharing them with him. But how could she express this? She'd never be able to voice her emotions accurately and yet with modesty. She reviewed the sentences running through her mind. They oscillated between stupidity, platitude, and trivial expertise in the field of performance.

She got dressed, deciding that it was better not to overstay her welcome, particularly since her overwhelming desire was to leave within the sheets of this bed the terrifying realization that something irreparable had taken place during the night, making her queasy.

Awake now, David invited her to keep him company in the bathroom. While he was shaving, Amélie, eager to test her heart's independence, delivered an awkwardly pompous lecture to the effect that their relationship could not go anywhere, there was no possibility of love between them, and that was that.

David promptly reassured her. He softened the import of the night, praising the merits of complicity. He proved conciliatory to the point of indifference, so that Amélie began to think she had dreamt his intense words of love, attributing to them a significance they never had.

CHAPTER TWO

*I*n the mass of helter-skelter sensations arising from this new adventure, Amélie noted a few striking facts: First, she was no longer hungry. From the moment of her meeting with David she experienced a curious kind of repletion, of indifference to food. Eating had become extra work, the way her appetite would vanish at the thought of seeing the dentist.

This sensation grew every time she was close to David. At the prospect of calling him, her throat dried, her voice sounded hoarse, her belly ached, she experienced nausea attacks. She cleared her throat before dialing his number, like a singer waiting in the wings to step out on the stage. She'd take in a large draft of air before meeting him, as though readying herself for a scuba diving plunge.

What she lost in appetite flourished as curiosity. She wanted to know everything about David: his past, his tastes, his habits, his political beliefs. She had always been curious about everything, particularly in relation to men. Their truth, nestled under the cover of propriety, or of an elegant suit, constituted an exciting enigma, a rebus. But desire had slipped in through the stitches of her curiosity, and her interest in David suddenly became an absolute necessity. Why? Were these the raptures of love? Or was it rather that, oppressed by the unseemliness of her desires, and her aroused voluptuousness, she made it her duty to find out all she could about the man who brought her to this pitch of erotic bliss? Damned if she knew!

David became the object of her assiduous study. His simplest sentences seemed to burst with allusions, shades of meaning. She spent every waking moment analyzing his silences, examining the nature of every intonation, every word, bringing to this scientific inquiry the dazzling ardor of a dilettante, finally aware, late in life, of her true vocation.

This passionate absorption was such fun that she mistook it at first for a wanton whim. Soon, however, she was forced to admit she had no choice in the matter: the investigation had to be completed. What was his opinion of makeup? Did he perchance dislike the expressions she was in the habit of using?

"Watch out! Be careful!" she told herself as she questioned her lover with the slyness of a racetrack gambler worming out a tip. She had to stay on her toes, doing her best to avoid any blunders and faux pas. She espoused his opinions to the point of servility: A drafty spot in a restaurant? No problem, she happened to feel hot. A steak for two? The very thing she was dying to share.

She felt deep within a childish, humiliating, annoying desire to do things right. Yet, despite all her efforts, a kind of uncertainty persisted, hooked to the dark, enigmatic panels of David's personality, like a whelk fastened to a rock. Did he love her? Did he think of her? What did he think of her?

An ambiguous word would fill Amélie with anxiety. She felt like a swivel-pin around which whirled unanswerable questions. No sooner did David calm her qualms, allowing her to think of something else, than she felt guilty of infidelity. And she went on worrying, or pretending to do so, as she expressed her amorous fears, as though this agitation proved her devotion.

Alerted by a scrap of common sense, Amélie tried hard to think: What did she feel for David? What did she expect of him? Physical pleasure? A bit of irresponsible happiness? The love of twin spirits? Because she wanted to appeal to him, without knowing what she thought, or what she expected from him, Amélie gave herself license to carry on with her affair until she might see things clearly. She made of doubt her ally, deciding to brief a case without knowing its nature, or its importance.

David did not indulge in this kind of narcissism. He pulled out all the stops to seduce Amélie. That's the way he was. She fit his plans perfectly, the reserves of dash and vigor he could devote to her. He sent flowers, wrote poems, and made up all kinds of rituals in order to avoid thinking too much: he brushed his hair nervously, kept on changing his bedsheets, had his car washed before calling on her. An exceptional situation calls for unexpected behavior. He was in love, a changed man.

From ordinary strategist he became a tactician. He would launch one operation on top of the other, reflecting upon them after the event. He could turn his coat without batting an eyelid, in order to straighten out a false impression. He might challenge a restaurant bill, and then, haunted by the dread of being taken for a miser, he'd shower her with lavish gifts. Had he been too eager, he'd stand her up the next day.

Not given to gab, he would suddenly discourse with eloquence. He'd move on request from one register to the next, as a copyist goes from Cézanne to Rembrandt. He'd talk a blue streak saying nothing, finding the right intonations and formulaic expressions for each circumstance. It was for the sake of alleviating Amélie's anxieties, to fill in blanks when the conversation lagged, and gaps in an affair that he feared might be cut short.

In sum, he was bending over backward simply to please her. But his plan of action was set, and that's what counted. He would pleasure her in bed, entertain her over the telephone, make her laugh over dinner. He'd make life beautiful and easy so that their liaison would seem innocuous. He wanted her open, dilated, creamy, as she was, with her thighs spread wide apart. Gradually, he'd prevail.

They shared fits of uncontrollable laugher, and tender feelings. Amélie took David to her favorite candy store in Montmartre, A la Mère de Famille; she introduced him to marshmallows, praline caramels, apple rock candy, aniseed cookies. David made faces, sickened by this surfeit of sweets. He got back at her, taking her to a poolroom where she scoffed at the green wool covering the tables, the ivory balls. In short, they put themselves out for each other. And their meetings acquired the joyous hue of a musical comedy.

CHAPTER THREE

*D*avid did not speak much of his childhood. The Orient oozed from the music of his phrasing, his untimely invocations of Allah, but he claimed to be French, unaware of the imperceptible condescension of the elegant Parisians whom he thought to be his friends. One day, recalling the city where he was raised, he suggested to Amélie:

—What if we left for Marrakech on Friday?

She began to plan at once the excuse she'd use to leave Paris for a weekend. She'd manage. She was good at lying without stammering or blushing, the aplomb of experience, no doubt . . . Deception had been part of her daily life for a long time, even before her meeting with David, before she ever had anything to hide.

She had never liked accounting for her schedule. In the evening, when she'd come home later than usual, she would say she had gone to the movies, when in actual fact she had been at the beauty parlor. She would then tell the story of the film, praise the acting, express her reservations as to the scenario. Of course this meant she had to go to the movies often enough, to nourish her memory and fill out her previous comments. She went with pleasure when her husband was away, in the evening, or on weekends. When he returned he would inquire about what she had done, and she'd describe her walks through the Bagatelle gardens of the Bois de Boulogne, or her meandering through the showrooms of the auction house of Drouot. She had to keep a careful record of her fibs to avoid telling the same story twice.

She did not want to dupe or betray anyone; she simply marked with her secrets the borders of her private territory, as animals do by spraying it with their urine. The span of her imagination encompassed vast areas; to her, truth was elastic, as malleable as a toothpaste tube. She played with it by hiding it under layers of silence, modifying it to her taste. Sometimes she took the liberty of reinventing it.

Beauty parlors were a source of inspiration. She enjoyed their stealthy softness, which instigated confessions, and the sweet perfume of hair spray. She tried a number of them, singling out two. The first was a den of old ladies who kept on praising the use of corsets and stretch hose. Amélie introduced herself as a housewife who suspected her husband of infidelity. The hair stylist was a middle-aged woman in her forties, with unshaven armpits, and a thick, tightly laced waist. A wide belt pushed the folds of her flesh upward toward her breasts, and down in the direction of her hips. Thus encumbered, she was sparing of her movements, but bossed her clients around. "Come on, Mrs. Martin, are you going to complain until you're blue in the face? Your grandson will come visit you. Mark my word."

She dispensed clever advice. The old bags expressed their opinions. The beauty parlor came to life with memories, stratagems to keep the straying husband. Everyone agreed as to male fickleness. Amélie left the shop feeling comforted.

The following week she'd go to the other beauty parlor. There she posed as a secretary who lived in hope of her employer's marriage proposal. The place, however, always startled her, suggesting a cushy bordello with its pink curtains, black-lacquered table-tops, and gilded brass wall sconces. Teetering on spike-heeled pumps, the young assistants, covered by see-through smocks, aped the icy, formal airs of the well-born, while the older hair stylists exchanged mocking remarks with overdressed clients. The advice Amélie got was to be a bit less naive. She'd sail out of there, her hair teased and blown, looking for all the world like a soufflé.

Her affair with David, though fruitful in opportunities to exercise her special gifts, seemed to have dampened her imagination instead of stimulating it. No longer did she lie joyously. Hard-pressed, she made do with approximations that cut her to the quick. "You're in a slump!" she'd say to herself, mourning the good old days when her fibs provided the safety valves required by her imagination. Reduced to the function of alibis, they had been stripped of their panache, not to mention their subversive charm. They were part and parcel of her conjugal duties, a proof of her good manners, like a bread-and-butter note. There was no fun in it any longer.

*F*riday, 1 P.M. David prevailed to have Amélie occupy a window seat, as though her introduction to Morocco was to begin on the Orly runway. "At last," he sighed with relief, getting into his seat. They were leaving Paris, where Amélie remained reserved, circumspect as soon as he broached the subject of the future. He couldn't hold this against her. How could she possibly react any other way a few streets away from her children and husband?

Beyond the Strait of Gibraltar, everything could change. He would feel stronger, like a conquering hero. On his home ground he could convince her. The magic quality of the city, the lavish wedding feast to which he was taking her this very evening should prove irresistible.

The scent of cologne-saturated washcloths spread throughout the airplane. Amélie listening gleefully to the light clatter of the safety belt buckles being snapped shut, the slamming of the luggage racks overhead. Traveling delighted her, freeing her of the burden of time. Time became relative: fast at the ticket counter, drawn-out and slow in the lounge at the gate. During the flight it seemed regulated by a stopwatch, revealing its disconcerting reliance on convention by the jet lag following arrival.

The flight to Marrakech was nonstop. Too bad. She also liked ports of call. Thus discovered by pure chance, the world was made to order for her. Every bit of it was tamed: its waiting rooms, its runways. She deciphered the alphabet of the customs placards. With the universe shrinking she expanded.

Ensconced in her seat next to David, Amélie was babbling happily, like a child on a school holiday, celebrating the promising start of what her husband thought was "a professional symposium."

David interrupted her chatter:

—When I see your lips moving, all I think of is how much I want you.

24

—Let's check it out . . . , she said, gauging the lump rising in his jeans.

—Don't touch me! he threatened, stressing each syllable.

Taking his virulence for a compliment, Amélie went on talking. Conscious of the sensuous motion of her lips, of the outline of her breasts under her blouse, her languid thighs upon the seat, she became an exhibitionist, for the sole pleasure of watching David engrossed by her least significant gestures. However, his stare was as disquieting as a clock that had suddenly stopped ticking, when he interrupted her again:

—I'd like to spread your legs, lick your cunt. I'd bare your clitoris with my tongue, roll it between my lips.

He was speaking in an almost inaudible voice. On purpose. Amélie had to lean forward in order to hear him, picking up the scent of his desire, feeling his breath upon her skin. He wanted her to discard her liveliness close to indifference, needed to hold her attention, to make her yield to his will. Amélie's nostrils were palpitating; she had stopped smiling. He knew he had won.

—I'd like to feel you come in my mouth, hear you cry out, see your eyes roll back, and penetrate far into you, for a long, long time, until you come again. Would you like that?

Reassured at the thought of being desired with such intensity, Amélie allowed herself to experience the tumult of her senses. David's raw desire aroused her. She cast a furtive look in the direction of the airline hostesses sitting at the back of the cabin, next to the facilities.

—Let's go, she suggested.

—No, wait. I want to take a long time fucking you . . .

As soon as they landed, David started speaking Arabic. Amélie began to feel she did not know him. These eructating and caressing inflections were like the lovemaking of a stranger. He had taken hold of both their passports, answering for her the customs officer's questions, checking that nothing was missing from their luggage, and that the driver sent by his friends had arrived. She would have to get used to depending on him.

The hotel was not far. She gazed at the Atlas mountains, taking in the scenery through the car windows. But what really worried her was the thought of running into an acquaintance in the hall of the newly renovated and fashionable hotel where he was taking her. Her hat and sunglasses could hardly ensure her anonymity. She was too well aware of the pleasure of gossip, the sense of power it gave those who detained a secret and passed it on. She had to be wary of a possible witness.

They walked up the steps of an ocher-colored building, framed by a white sugar-like glaze, entered the central hall where the reception desk could be observed by each and every one. The desk clerk suggested that Amélie sit down, probably judging the formalities to be too masculine or tiring for her. She spurned this suggestion, her eyes sweeping the vestibule as for a wide-angle shot.

David was enumerating the names of his illustrious Moroccan protectors, stressing his own prominence to a visibly impressed desk clerk. Amélie took in this scene with growing amazement, disillusioned by the tasteless lack of manners that prompted her lover to blow his own horn in front of an employee.

Embarrassed, Amélie would have liked to distance herself from her companion. Not to mention that the longer they lingered at the reception desk, the greater her risk of running into an acquaintance. However, her next thought was one of self-criticism: Her reaction was snobbish, conventional, contemptible! David had a curious sense of panache. So what? Didn't she have the guts to acknowledge who and what he was? Taking up the challenge, she snuggled up to him with partisan defiance, ready to shoot anyone who might judge him as mercilessly as she had just done.

Actually there was no guilty party, quite the opposite. David's method was efficient, perfectly in keeping with his country's code. The hotel's director materialized instantly from his office, as though summoned by this client's importance. He shook David's hand obsequiously. He went so far as to accompany them to their floor.

The room overlooking the ramparts was large. The director left them bowing and scraping, after showing them the switch to the air conditioner, the minibar, and the hiding place of the wall safe. He drew the special attention of the floor personnel to the presence of this client who had just confirmed his quality by giving a large tip. While Amélie was reading the guide sheet to the services offered by the hotel, an uninterrupted ballet of valets began. They were carrying in mint tea, flowers, pastry, and bath salts. Allah's name was ever present as servants greeted the master while he dispensed munificent tips.

Finally this hullabaloo died down, leaving silence in its wake. As for David, he was renewing his immemorial connections with the perfumes, words, habits of his childhood. His face glowed with joy. Awed, Amélie could not overcome a passivity she knew to be absurd. Guilty of having disavowed him, she awaited his forgiveness, and his initiative. She expected him to take her in his arms.

However, David drifted toward the bathroom. Regretfully, she watched him withdraw, heard water running from a faucet. Judging by the flow's noisy power, she concluded it had to be that of the bathtub. Suddenly he was standing by her side. He led her away without a word. Seated on the tub's edge, face-to-face with her, he looked at her harshly. Now she was certain of having hurt his feelings. He must have sensed her sudden coolness, and wondered why she had withdrawn her hand from his as they arrived at the hotel. She was about to apologize.

Slowly David unbuttoned her blouse, slipped it off without taking his eyes off her. He swiveled her around to unhook her bra. Then he turned off the faucets. He was breathing hard as his fingers skimmed over her skirt's zipper, as though he wished to strip her without touching her skin. She was naked now, and he turned her so that once again she faced him. His eyes moved over her body, as though to imprint upon his retina the shadows and curves of her flesh. Delicately, like a minuet dancer, he took her by the hand to help her step into the warm tub. "Of course," she said to herself, as David removed the soap from its wrapper. It was all so simple she didn't even think it through: David meant nothing sexual. All he wanted was to bathe her.

He began with her hands, her arms; then her feet and legs. Methodically, he enclosed in his fist each of Amélie's hands, ran his middle finger between her toes. Next he reached her neck, her shoulders, so intent on what he was doing, so close to Amélie's skin, that their eyes never met.

Amélie knelt in the tub so he could soap her belly and breasts. She was relieved not to have to face his ill humor. Yet she was also disappointed. Could it be that David's impen-

etrable air held no mystery? Too bad! Might as well let herself grow numb in warm water, enjoying his chaste caresses.

She wondered at his intentions when he began to suck
on her breasts, drawing back to contemplate the reddened,
erect nipples with the satisfied smile of an artist coaxing a new
aggressiveness from his work. Next his hands approached the
contours of her cunt. He ordered:

—Turn around!

She offered him a submissive rump. Stimulated by the
long wait, the unexpected, she held her breath. David's fingers,
gleaming with soap, insinuated themselves into the groove
between her buttocks. He enclosed her pussy in the palm of
his hand, penetrated it with his thumb, gently stroking the
dilated walls of her sex. She bit her lips in order to keep from
moaning: perhaps he was simply playing with her. He was
capable of cutting things short at this point, were he certain of
having achieved what he sought.

—Come with me, he said.

He helped her step out of the tub, and, having carefully
dried her with a soft bath towel, laid her down on the living
room sofa. Amélie wanted him so desperately, she felt an abyss
opening up between her legs. Instead of taking her, David
began to peel some fruit. She begged him to make love to her,
but all he did was feed her small morsels, bird-style. He
claimed he loved to watch her eat, filling her mouth with tan-
gerine slices and sweets. Bewildered, Amélie kept quiet. She
knew she had lost her bearings, not sure whether his little game
was over, or had not even begun.

—My sweet, you know I love you more than anything
in the world? he announced.

Unable to guess what he was getting at, Amélie remained silent, awaiting his next sentence.

—This evening I could take you to my goddaughter's wedding, but I don't wish to do so.

She stared at him in amazement. He went on:

—I'm divorced; we are not engaged. If you come with me this evening you'll be taken for an escort girl. I love you too much to introduce you to my friends under such conditions. You understand?

—Of course I do. Never mind, my love. I'll be just fine here. I'll wait for you peacefully.

David's explanation satisfied her, and she was relieved at the thought of not having to face a crowd of foreigners with strange ways.

—I haven't brought you here to drop you. Who do you take me for? Leila, my goddaughter, the one who is getting married this evening, is coming to the hotel beauty parlor to have her hair done . . .

—I don't see what it has to do with us . . . , Amélie retorted. She was exasperated by David's incomprehensible train of thought, and even more so by the manner in which he addressed her, as though she were an illiterate moron.

—I called her from Paris to set things up. She'll come for you around five, after her hairdresser appointment. She'll take you to her home, where she'll introduce you as a friend from Paris come by surprise to her wedding. I'll get there at eight, as part of the male contingent of the wedding procession. You'll see. It's a magnificent spectacle!

—But I don't want you to leave me alone! she cried out overcome by panic. What shall I tell them if they ask me how

I met her, how long have we known one another, that kind of thing.

David burst out laughing, certain she was putting on an act. She wasn't. Amélie's vivid imagination was filled at this moment by harems oozing with kohl, overflowing with Turkish delight, and all the stories read or heard about women taken advantage of by apparently civilized, moderate Moslems.

—Listen, say as little as possible. You'll be just fine.

As much as Amélie enjoyed the gratuitous telling of tall tales, she did not care to lie under duress. She felt David was ordering her life without consulting her. He had imagined this scenario on his own, without ever thinking she had a contribution to make, or envisioning the charming possibility of a shared imposture. It had never crossed his mind. She, who measured her respect for others by the quality of the elaborate lies she spun for them, felt humiliated, scorned. David was treating this little comedy in a trifling manner; he had bungled it. Moreover, he expected to be applauded!

—Wait a minute! Tell me if I'm wrong. Your idea is that I'll be a member of the wedding of someone I don't know, while pretending not to know you?

—Leila will come to your rescue. She'll introduce you to people . . . She's a love of a girl, and so beautiful. She's had a crush on me since she was a kid.

Amélie was about to regurgitate this twaddle when the doorbell rang. It was Leila, arriving promptly at five. Disheveled, still in her robe, Amélie saw a honey-skinned siren barge into the room and throw herself in David's arms. Looking her over, Leila was aghast at Amélie's lack of style, but she soon recovered, and even seemed happy to note that her rival paled by comparison. A radiant beauty, bursting with health, Leila introduced herself, then suggested a bit archly that Amélie might have to change for the wedding.

Generally methodical and self-controlled, Amélie felt a lump of anguish and jealousy rise in her throat. Having lost her composure, she was incapable of any efficient action. She could not locate the right color bra, nor the indispensable shoulder pads for her elegant silk shirt. Moreover, her only pair of black panty hose was marred by a run.

She despised herself for failing to be radiantly lovely, able to shake Leila's self-confidence even for a moment. Then she tried to reason herself out of this frame of mind. She was behaving like a kid. After all, she was nothing but bother for this young woman on her wedding day. Having more or less pulled herself together, she crammed her makeup kit into her handbag, together with the bra she had finally located. She felt unable to deal with her irrational fears: humiliated by David's total casualness, she felt like a schoolgirl, abandoned by her family to the mother superior of a boarding school. Just before leaving, a grandiloquent David whispered in her ear:

—Tonight, my love, remember my eyes will be making love to you amid the crowd. We probably won't be able to speak. But there's no need for words to reach an understanding.

Skeptical yet reassured by the loving inflections of David's voice, Amélie followed Leila into her grey coupe. She was dazzling, intimidating, with her henna-tinted hands, her heavy braided chignon studded with pearls.

—Am I wearing too much makeup? she inquired, suddenly humanly nervous.

They entered the house through kitchens humming with activity. The floor was cluttered with bric-a-brac, cauldrons, sideboards littered with mess and filth. Everything was topsy-turvy. The palace's backyard was a pigpen of crockery, copper pots, and dishes. Railed at on arrival by hysterical women at the end of their rope, Leila led Amélie up the stairs to the second floor. She introduced her to her sisters standing on the landing:

—This is Amélie, a friend from Paris. We'll have to find her a caftan. Farida, would you take care of this?

Amélie did not know where to go, who to follow. Unable to make up her mind, she was standing there when five fat crones, wearing white baggy dresses, let out strident ululations. Their curled tongues moved swiftly against the roof of their mouths, while their eyes acquired a glassy stare, an expression of concentrated indifference. Their tanned skins were leathery, their faces dotted with suture-like kohl markings. They were singing the praises of the future bride. Leila protested: "That's too much. They've taken to following me everywhere I go!"

They handed Amélie a violet caftan adorned with moiré patterns she deemed frightful. Following the flow of people coming and going, she found herself in a bathroom crammed with women. No one in that cackling henhouse paid her the least attention. Amélie put on the cumbersome gown, whose innumerable small buttons required reserves of patience, and whose hem made her trip. No doubt she lacked experience, so far as she could gauge by the dexterity of her fellow prisoners. Bundled up in this shapeless vestment, which made her look insipid, she knew that in comparison with the Oriental women crowded around her she did not possess an iota of style.

Leila appeared in the frame of the door, inquiring as to the hospitality that had been extended to her. One glance and she knew what was needed:

—You've got to have a belt, she decreed.

Amélie thanked her, assured her that she felt wonderful. Gradually the bathroom was emptying of people. Amélie found herself alone with Sophie, Leila's French friend, a pretty blonde who approached her with the good-natured frankness of girls who feel good about themselves. "I'm getting old," Amélie told herself as she listened to the girl's account of her course of studies, and her boyfriends. What could she possibly say to Sophie? Perhaps tell her age to mark a distance. She could not mention her children, her husband, least of all David. She had outgrown the age of dressing-room confessions. Sophie began to question her:

—How long have you known Leila?

—Not very long . . .

—How and where did you meet her? Was it in Paris?

—Yes, in Paris, at the home of mutual friends. Amélie was groping for a way to end this conversation.

Clearly, filling out the loose bits of information to make her story more believable was of no use. Sophie obviously knew all about her affair with David: she hinted with the ridiculous pride some people derive from their intimacy with the rich and famous that she was Leila's sole and most effective confidante. Best to cut this short.

Announced by the rumbling of drums, the men's procession was starting on the ground floor. Magnificent-looking in spite of his slicked-down hair, an unfortunate habit of his when she was not around to tousle it, David pretended not to recognize her when their eyes met. That's what she'd been afraid of. The silent complicity he had promised her had vanished at the very first glance. Only the emptiness of the evening lay ahead.

Amélie took note of the beauty of the women, the pleasure the men took in displaying their own importance. However, she didn't have the detachment required for an anthropological analysis. Alone in the crowd, surrounded by empty space, she felt vulnerable.

She had the impression of being on exhibit, like a statue. She sought some consolation from her thoughts: Were she to choose her place in a museum, she knew now she'd prefer to disappear amid *The Bourgeois of Calais,* rather than star alone as *The Thinker*. Indifferent, curious, appraising or critical glances seemed to lose their sharpness when spread out across a crowd.

She moved about, unable to listen to the orchestra, or take part in the meal. What's the point of dancing without your partner, of eating without your table companion? All at once, she noticed the bride's sisters. They were whispering and pointing at her. Curiosity or ill will? Her discomfort turned to humiliation. She imagined the gossip passing from one to the other: Wasn't she the mistress of their dear uncle, the very one they had to pretend not to know anything about? If he had planned to protect her reputation, he had most certainly failed: She was presently the chief piece of gossip of the evening. His insistence on ignoring her presence was a disastrous move. With the whole family in the know, it began to look like a disclaimer.

She tried to reason with herself without feeling persecuted, when in reality she moved surrounded by general indifference. She sought a quiet corner to spend the rest of the evening. Seated on a sofa, she realized that, restful as this position was, it failed to set her mind at rest. The least look inflicted a wound.

The only solution was to keep moving. She had to bestir herself. There was nothing suspicious about her shifting from place to place. One could assume she was looking for friends, getting something to drink, going to the bathroom. She got a glimpse of David. High on booze and old friendships, he exulted, ogling pretty women, lavishing manly embraces on his old pals. Was she jealous? she wondered. Certainly not. She did not even pine to join him. At this moment she hated him.

She gave herself up to the wicked pleasure of dissecting him, making mincemeat out of him. He thought only of himself! He wanted her at his beck and call, as the mirror image of his own demeanor.

He claimed to know the ingredients necessary to her happiness; she needed him, craved his reassuring presence, his strength, his ability to make decisions. This certainty, his belief in the cliché that women need to depend on men, allowed him to avoid thinking of her as a complex, ever-changing individual. He did not have to put himself in her place. Since he only harbored good feelings toward her, he was convinced that he fulfilled her just as much. It went without saying. No need, then, to look at her in the course of the evening. Having glimpsed her, he had emitted signs of a joyful complicity he actually shared only with himself. If she were drowning under his very eyes, he would no doubt have winked at her in merry encouragement.

Amélie was tired; she felt out of place amid the frenetic rhythm of this triumphant feast. Far from everyone's gaze, she locked herself up in the second-floor bathroom. Erasing from her face the fixed smile she'd been wearing all evening, she burst into tears and fell asleep. Upon awakening, she observed on her cheek the mark left by the bath sheet she had used as a pillow. It provided a fine excuse for not returning at once to the ground floor. She was going to linger just where she was until recovering a human face, and freshening her makeup. Thereupon, a host of cockroaches invaded the room. Trembling with disgust, she changed her mind and joined the party.

By half past twelve, she had memorized every detail of the reception rooms: paintings, furniture, carpets . . . Leaning on a sideboard, glass in hand, she wondered what profit she might possibly derive from this wedding party. She felt like an ordinary clerk teetering on the brink of incompetence. She had covered the party like a dutiful tourist visiting one Roman ruin after another. Now she was running low, like a car on empty. Moreover, her feet were killing her.

However, it was still early, too early to tell David she wanted to go. She indulged in higher mathematics: Having left at five in the afternoon, she had just completed seven and a half hours of presence, whereas David, who came three hours later, had barely concluded four and a half hours of fun. "All right! Let's see now . . ." she told herself, trying to catch her breath in the middle of a train of thought that augured complications as tricky as the math problems of her childhood. One of them, she recalled with a shudder, was about measuring water outflow within a given time span from some putative faucet. She pondered: "Considering that a successful dinner party lasts four hours (between eight-thirty and half past twelve), I must endure another hour for David to feel he really partied. Let's call it fifty minutes!" she concluded, pleased with the time cut she had secured for herself.

At a quarter to one, the exhilarated assembly was suddenly seized in a swirling motion that Amélie compared to weather forecasts: "Morning mists and passing storms . . . ," or the pilot's warning: "Fasten your seat belts. Turbulence ahead!" She cast herself in the role of a meteorologist looking into the eye of a cyclone, and found herself face-to-face with David:

—What's up?

Regretfully diverting his attention from a moving silhouette, David answered:

—That's the crown prince. He's just left an official dinner party to congratulate Leila in person.

—Oh, she replied simply.

—Don't tell me you didn't notice all the body-guards!

He was scolding her. His tone filled Amélie with rage.

—I can't take it anymore, she hissed. I'm leaving. Where can I find a taxi?

Taken aback, David changed his tune. He regretted his bad-tempered attitude.

—It's out of the question. I'll come with you, of course. I'll join you in the car after I've said goodbye.

Amélie rushed upstairs to remove her caftan and find her handbag. Now that her patient waiting had come to an end, she savored the haste that was part and parcel of her Parisian way of life. Her joy, her renewed flow of energy made her realize how much the evening had depressed her.

Her relief pinpointed the distress, eclipsed at times during the party by rancor and boredom. She had experienced this bewilderment much as one does happiness, without questioning her state of mind. Its obviousness struck her at the very moment she no longer felt it. It had become as dim as a fading memory, leaving her full of doubts as to having ever endured it.

She left the palace as she had arrived, through the kitchens. The night was pleasantly cool, lit by torches, the street cluttered with limos and bodyguards. Stopping on the sidewalk, Amélie pondered where to go next. However, the driver recognized her, and, rushing over, helped her into his car.

—Monsieur will be out any moment, she declared, looking at her watch.

The well-trained chauffeur drove up to the portal. Amélie gathered her scattered feelings, focusing her attention on the walnut door, with the impatience of a lotto player staring at the numbers on the colorful balls.

The guests were leaving the reception. Trustful at first, she kept on the lookout for David, hoping with every surging silhouette that it was he. This time the wait sapped her optimism.

The scenario was repeating itself. Bursts of laughter; the slamming of car doors. David's driver would start the car, parking it on the sidewalk to allow the guests determined to call it a night drive past him. Then, putting it in reverse, he'd place it at the tail end of the car line. Sorely afflicted by these deceptive departures, these about-face turns. Amélie no longer knew what was more unbearable, David's disregard of her patient expectation, or the chauffeur's discrediting her reckless announcement of David's imminent arrival.

However, she gave up the idea of setting deadlines beyond which she'd have to take action. Better wait. Inside the car it was warm, and she could sleep.

David arrived fifty minutes later. He apologized. Leila had prevented him from leaving . . .

Back at the hotel, he couldn't stop praising the magnificence of the décor, the quality of the orchestra, his pleasure in being with old friends:

—Did you see the buffet . . . and the crowd! The Home Secretary was there and so was the chief of protocol . . .

What a kid he is, thought Amélie, who had not shared his pleasure in rubbing shoulders with the kingdom's crème de la crème.

—You must have seen me, on Khaled's right during the procession! No wonder I was shown due respect. I'm his father's friend and executor, after all!

Amélie had stopped listening: could David possibly mistake this monologue for conversation? He did not even try to make amends for his pitiful lack of talent as a storyteller.

"Me, me, me!" she muttered under her breath while removing her makeup in the bathroom.

"This man thinks only of himself, speaks only of himself! He could have wondered how I was spending the evening. Nothing doing!" There were two possibilities: throw a fit, but, having looked forward to these two days, she could hardly change them into a catastrophe; her other option was silence. She chose the latter.

David was stretched out over the mattress when she joined him in the room. Taken aback by his posture, Amélie stopped, embarrassed not to recall which side of the bed was his. Pretending to look for something so as to gain some time, she envisioned the topography of his Paris studio, comparing the orientation of his bed to this one. She climbed submissively onto the left side, as though nothing were the matter and these computations unnecessary.

Half past three in the morning. Holding her in his arms David fell sound asleep. Lying on her side, her knee imprisoned between David's legs, Amélie was unable to catch a wink. She tried to break free, loosen his grip in order to rest on her back.

However careful, her crawling movements annoyed the sleeping man who grunted some kind of ultimatum in response to her persistent struggle. His limbs, petrified by sleep, forced Amélie to assume the curve of his body by immobilizing her in a somnambulistic grip.

At six in the morning, David pulled open the curtains, then thrust the French windows wide open to step out on the balcony. Exhausted, stiff and aching, Amélie blinked in the dazzling sunlight. She tried to detect the joke in his maneuver, as a child reads something playful in a dog's determination to bite him.

—What are you doing?

—I'm getting up, don't you see, he answered calmly, walking toward the bathroom. I'm going to shower.

Amélie sat up in bed, her throat tight with the hate she felt for their first morning. All remnants of sleepiness had vanished. The abscess formed last night by disappointment and rancor had grown into a phlegm. Her instant, sharp, mechanical, irrepressible reaction was like the report of an automatic pistol. She grabbed her robe at the foot of the bed, and burst into the bathroom shouting:

—David, are you going to tell me why you brought me here if you made up your mind not to pay me the least bit of attention?

—What are you talking about? he answered, seemingly amazed.

—I'll tell you what I'm talking about. Since our arrival you've been treating me like a disposable tissue. I was dreaming of spending this weekend with you. And all you do is hand me over to strangers at a party where I'm bored stiff. And not once have you given a thought about my feelings! You hardly said goodnight to me. And now that you're no longer sleepy, you have the nerve to wake me up to take your shower!

—What do you mean? Was Leila unkind to you?

—That's not the problem! You're the problem. You treat me like a piece of shit! The only thing I want to do is to get out of here! Get it?

—But that's impossible, Amélie! I love you.

—Well, what would it be like if you didn't?

—No, wait. This is much too serious. Come, sit down. I want us to talk this over.

—But I am talking to you now, David! And believe me, for what I have to say, I don't really need to sit down.

This brief fit of verve left Amélie with a heavy heart and a mind empty of the resounding, blazing, bedizened insults that might have dispelled her spite. With nothing more to add, she burst into tears. These forced-out tears were followed by others, which, in turn, propelled new fits. Soon this autonomous activity was beyond her control. Unable to repress her sobs, she let herself go, her nose red with weeping, her eyes swollen. David took her in his arms.

—Hush! Come with me.

He sat her down on the living-room sofa.

— Amélie, my love . . . Calm down. I'm sorry. I never realized that you were frightened of going with Leila. I thought you were kidding. It's your fault, you know. You always look so sure of yourself.

—You're joking, aren't you?

—Not one bit, I swear. You look so beautiful, so independent . . . I thought you'd find a Moroccan wedding a fun thing to do, that you'd exercise your critical sense, make me laugh by telling me what you thought of it all . . .

He stopped pacing the floor, came toward her.

—You're just a child, my love, and I didn't realize it . . . I love you even more. Maybe you do need me, after all.

Listening to David, Amélie realized he had once again turned the situation to his advantage. She had the definite impression of witnessing a conjurer's act to which she could not fathom the trick. She held back, reluctant to lose her temper, as she breathed the foul air of specious arguments, bad faith, and stupidity creeping in between his words. Either David was shamelessly manipulative, or he actually believed what he was saying, which was even worse; but she did not wish to think about it, even less to discuss it.

He grew impatient:

—Do you really believe I never once looked your way? I saw nothing *but* you, thought of no one else the whole time! At dinner I even looked for you, but you had vanished . . .

His tone softened again:

—Sweetheart, I don't want you to go; please stay, I need you.

Amélie was catching her breath, still impeded by her tears.

— Amélie, I didn't give a damn about this wedding. I wanted to show you the place where I grew up, because I love you. Had I known it would be like this I would never have taken you with me . . . I feel terrible. I should have known . . .

Now that her tears were dry, Amélie wished to put an end to this pitiful scene, which was becoming redundant. David's display of remorse clearly signaled the only way to end their fight: to be merry, comfort him, reestablish his good mood.

—Let's call a truce! Shall we stop now?

—I really hate myself, he said. What a bloody fool I've been!

—Stop! Let's call it quits, David, shall we? She suggested with a smile: Let's order breakfast. I'm hungry. I had nothing to eat last night.

She burst out laughing before he had a chance to bring up the subject of her abstinence.

—I take back what I just said . . . Let's just say I'm hungry . . . Come, embrace me, show me how much you love me, kiss me.

David's tread was heavy as he walked over and gave her a penitent kiss.

—Can't you do better than that? she whispered in his ear.

She opened her negligee, setting about to drown David's remorse in a kaleidoscope of sensations whose effectiveness she gauged by the stiffness of his cock, letting him make the next move.

David could feel his anxiety spreading to some moving, undefinable center, while Amélie's eloquent body drove away the specter of a possible break-up. He was both relieved and tense, burdened still by the accumulation of energy summoned in the course of their fight.

His sharpened excitement was tinged with fury. So the moment had come to make amends, to erase the memory of his presumed lack of sensitivity, to eliminate it altogether by his gifted lovemaking. He'd outdo himself! Under the cover of civility he would prolong the gallant foreplay, making Amélie bemoan his excess of amorous technique, which filled her with desire as sharp as needles.

He drew her into the bedchamber, lay her down upon the bed, and leaned over her body. He brushed her skin lightly, caressing her with the back of his wrist, his warm breath between his lips. When she tried to touch him, he drew back. This form of punishment excited him. He took a firm hold of her wrists, signifying that she'd better behave, licked with his wet, rough tongue her neck, the furrow of her groin, the hollow of her elbows. Then he turned her over on her stomach, scratching his morning beard upon her thighs and buttocks.

Amélie panted, writhing and crushing between her fingers the tails of the bedsheets she pulled from under the mattress. David's caresses aroused her, as did the role she was supposed to play. She thought at first that she could shake his resolve: pretending to struggle against him, she lifted up her ass, spread her legs, and let him see and covet her iridescent vulva. She imagined David's eyes lighting up her cunt like a projector, heating it up, making it blush like a girl. She'd have given anything to check his look, gauge his prick.

Intractable, he did not take her. She played the game, emitted doleful sounds, threw imploring looks. Nothing doing! Then she capitulated, begged:

—Please, please, David, fuck me!

Amélie's expectation made David white-hot. Her stratagems and surrender had driven him to the edge. He took her.
The skillfully restrained thrusts of her loins finally uprooted
his resentment. He climaxed inside her.

She woke up before him. She had slept in his tightly
clinched embrace, without feeling the slightest tickle or teas-
ing provocation of his body hair upon her skin. Nor had she
tried to disengage their bodies from one another. She looked
at him, smiled. Like a child sucking its thumb he was holding
her cunt in the palm of his hand, a token of ownership.

—Is it late? he inquired, opening one eye.

—Twelve-fifteen.

—What should we do? Order breakfast, or go out to
lunch? he suggested.

—Let's go out. I haven't seen anything of this city.

The air was dry, the sun shone gently on the front steps
of the hotel. David turned down the porter's suggestion of a
large or small taxi. Taking Amélie by the hand, he helped her
up into one of the numerous horse-drawn open calèches, and
gave the directions to the driver.

Glutted with sleep and pleasure, Amélie was no longer
concerned with keeping their affair secret. It was brazenly
exposed in this outpost for all to see. David savored the ride
wordlessly. They left the Gueliz, heading for the minaret of
the mosque of Koutoubiya, the most beautiful monument of
Marrakech, and the medina. Amélie was famished by the time
they reached the great square, Djemaa-el-Fna, situated in the
middle of the city. They settled down to lunch in the shade of
a straw roof held up by poles. It was a typical greasy spoon, but
they served delicious brochettes. Later they walked through

narrow alleys, protected by cloth roofs under the sun. The light fell in stripes over the vendors of <u>babouches</u>, exotic fabrics, and all manner of trimmings.

Night was falling on the square as they issued from the labyrinth of narrow streets. The snake charmers, monkey-trainers, musicians, and storytellers had arrived, adding a picturesque element to the din, the crowd's restless commotion.

They returned arm in arm. Back at the hotel, no sooner was the question of getting dressed for dinner raised, than they glanced shyly away, embarrassed by the sudden glimpse of marital life opening up before their eyes. They chose solitary ablutions, each in turn locked up in the bathroom, as though they wished to keep the creation of their allure a secret.

David retired to the bathroom, while Amélie dressed in the bedroom. She unsealed the tissue-paper containing the silk stockings she had selected for their delicate, rustling sheen, just as she had chosen her black bikini panties for their revealing crotch, her garter belt for its corsetlike effect and her black push-up bra for the way it enhanced her cleavage. "Pretty good . . . ," she rejoiced, preening herself in the closet's full-length mirror.

David burst in as she bent over the desk to toss the wrappings into the waste-paper basket. "I've forgotten to—" he muttered, stopping in mid-sentence at the sight of Amélie's fanny and the strips of her pale, naked skin swathed in black silk. He took a few steps forward.

Amélie held her breath, arching her loins. She had no desire to look behind her, to watch David's approach, to recognize him. His heavy tread, laden with lust, could be that of any stranger, whose sexual vigor and kinky demands she was about to discover. He grabbed her hips, pushing aside the flaps of his bathrobe to glue his stomach to her rump, nestling between her black-girdled buttocks.

—Your ass is quite something . . . You're giving me horny ideas standing like that.

Amélie did not move. Goaded by her passivity, David slipped off her panties, sliding them down her thighs. Prick grasped in his fist like a painter's brush, he swept her wet, shimmering slit with the tip of his cock, whitewashing her vulva from clitoris to asshole.

—If you don't tell me to stop, he hissed, I'm going to fuck you in the ass. But first I want to hear you come.

Amélie did not say a word. Relishing David's breathless, menacing intentions, she bent over the desk, propped up by her elbows. He thrust the entire length of his rod into her snatch, again and again, one long stroke after the other, before rubbing the head of his penis against the moist opening of her cunt. Like the surge of high tide, his rhythm grew thick and fast. Amélie's ears were ringing, her vision blurred. She gasped, suffocating with pleasure, tilting her hips to meet each powerful assault, amplifying the impact of his cock delving deep into her pussy.

When he ordered her with a murmur:

—Come now!

She uttered a long, modulated shriek, wrenched from the pit of her gut. She emerged from orgasm, cunt racked by spasms, while David's saliva-drenched forefinger coerced the threshold to her ass. A blinding pain radiated from anus to spine as David rammed himself in. The diameter of his cock split her bowels open, shoving home through the stranglehold of her loins. Agony invaded her with the quick burn of fire.

—Wait, she begged him, please, wait . . . Slower!

He paused.

—Do you want me to stop?

—No, go on. It hurts, but I like it. I don't quite know. Go on, but gently.

When he judged himself sufficiently lodged within her, David induced a to-and-fro motion to his prick trapped in the tightness of her shaft. At his first move, Amélie clenched her teeth, anticipating the same pain. But nothing prepared her for the violence of the sensation she now discovered. She howled, whitened knuckles gripping the sides of the desk.

Soon her pain subsided, diluted by the force of the tidal-wave hurling over her, flooding each and every nerve ending of her skin. David was invading her entrails. The giddiness inflicted upon her by his thrusts felt at once excruciating and delicious.

Through his cock, David perceived the onset of her pleasure, heralded by the surrender of her loins:

—But you like it, don't you? Say you love me fucking your ass!

—Yes! she cried out, I love it!

—I'm going to come! he bellowed.

He shoved himself in further, ejaculated, and Amélie felt her belly torn asunder by a climax that left her limp. They remained recumbent on the table, limbs askew like a pair of dislocated puppets. When he attempted to stand, she said:

—Don't leave me like this! I can hardly move, and I don't even know if I'll be able to sit down!

He laughed, gathered her into his arms, and carried her to the bed. Shivering, she slipped under the covers as David disappeared into the bathroom.

—My goodness! she exclaimed when he came back. You're all ready, spruced up and gorgeous! You're amazing. Look at me, I'm a wreck!

—I may seem fresh and relaxed, but I can hardly stand on my own two feet . . . Come on, darling, get ready, or we'll never get out of here in time for dinner. It's our last evening.

A limping Berber escorted them through the dark alleys of the medina, where the muffled sounds of the city, reduced to whisperings, seemed to stagnate. His lantern, burning with a night-light glow, softened the narrow streets teeming with shadows and, depending on his meandering path, projected haphazardly rays or bursts of light revealing doors, windows, vaguely, mouthlike humid orifices, carved in walls glossed by the penumbra.

Emerging from the labyrinth of primitive streets, Amélie felt she had traveled in time and space. They found themselves among the ordinary clients of a restaurant who stared at the newcomers as people do in pubs all over the world.

The ancient palace enclosed a square courtyard, sheltered by a makeshift velum. It was full of local color: Air drafts blew through the awnings, evoking the precariousness of desert tents, while a tinkling fountain seemed to orchestrate the smell of cinnamon and orange blossoms floating over the tables. They were placed face-to-face on deep sofas. David took Amélie's hand extended over a tablecloth covered with rose petals.

—I love you.

That's when she saw him: Jacques G., seated alone two tables away from theirs. His profile was too still to be natural. He had seen her, that was for sure! And he was still wondering whether he ought to recognize her. She lowered her head, pretending to rearrange the locks of hair falling over her forehead:

—Merde! she whistled between clenched teeth.

—What's the matter? David asked.

—Second table on the left; Jacques G., a friend of Paul's. He was on my right at our tenth anniversary party. What a disaster!

David said nothing; he felt responsible. It was he after all who had suggested Marrakech, keeping secret the fact that social collisions were far from uncommon in this exotic city. How stupid of him to have taken her to the city's best restaurant! But he was tired of racking his brain for obscure pubs in Paris where she wouldn't run into anyone she knew: African restaurants whose local color offset disastrous cuisine, charming bistros of the nineteenth arrondissement; touristy hash-houses of the Place du Tertre. Besides, there was something disturbing about watching her tremble with apprehension, overwhelmed by a physical malaise. It was more than inelegant, it was downright insulting! "It's her problem, after all!" he said to himself.

Amélie was clenching her fists, searching for the common-sense thing to do. She couldn't think straight, and this doubled her anxiety. She begged David to help her:

—David what am I going to do? What the hell can I do now?

—There are two possibilities: Either you pretend you haven't seen him, and he'll understand; or you greet him nicely, and he'll understand also.

Realizing the curtness of his suggestions, he added:

—Listen, your friend doesn't strike me as a fool. He's old enough to have found himself in such a situation before; he won't tell.

—You may be right, Amélie nodded dolefully. In fact, you're quite right. It's about time I regained some dignity. That's what you're hinting at, isn't it? So I'm going to say hello.

She lighted a cigarette and, taking advantage of the lack of an ashtray on the table, swept the room with her eyes in search of a busboy. Such an ostentatious move could only require social effusiveness:

—Oh, Jacques! Hello, how are you?

Jacques G. feigned surprise.

—Amélie, how wonderful to run into you!

Amélie noted that Jacques avoided looking at David. He proved himself circumspect, delicate, tactful; perhaps a bit tense. Their chat ended with a smile. She turned to David:

—Tell me, am I beet red?

—No, you handled it perfectly. I'm proud of you.

—All right! Shall we order our food now? He interrupted, forcing cheerfulness as he called the maître d' to their table.

She approved his suggestions without listening to them: salad, pigeon *pastilla,* couscous. The waiter took their order. Suddenly Amélie froze, as if some tiresome individual had covered her eyes with his hands, trumpeting: Guess who's here?

Martine L., her cousin, was coming out of the ladies' room heading straight for their table. Passing before them without seeing them, she was smiling across the room at someone on the left. She had just passed their table when her step grew hesitant.

Amélie saw her own image reflected in Martine's growing awareness. Resigned to a family scandal, she readied herself to put up a good front. Martine looked back all of a sudden, her face death-pale. Just as married as Amélie, she was having dinner with Jacques G. Amélie smiled at her with all the compassion she would have enjoyed finding a few moments ago in Jacques G. Martine returned her smile, relieved by this reaction in which she had failed just yet to detect the obligation of reciprocity.

Both couples isolated themselves in their respective bubbles of illegitimacy, circumscribed by the perimeter of their table. David questioned Amélie. She livened up, explained who Martine was, what Jacques G. did for a living. Together they appreciated the piquancy of the situation, commented on the toppling down of the probabilities of Jacques's indiscretions since their original analysis of the situation.

By dint of speaking of Paul, her husband, conjuring up memories, Amélie no longer felt at home at this table, with David. She was far from Paris, her center of gravity, and the disasters she was unleashing at this moment. She couldn't wait to get back home, avoid, circumvent, and snub these dire circumstances.

Amélie's terror was palpable, as was her desire to flee. Frustrated, hurt, deprived by the fugitive nature of her love, David attempted to hold her back, captivate her attention. But he did not possess a gift for conversation. He was a man of action, unskilled in playful repartee. "Might as well ask a skeptic to lead the séance table," he said to himself, disheartened. Drained by these one-way efforts, he was growing weary.

He alternated stories and silences. She listened vacantly to the first, unable to overcome the second. Both found themselves unable to compress the duration of the dinner, much like unmatched objects of different weights, ill-suited to prop up books upon a bookshelf. The wine was good; the dishes followed one another. They sampled the food on their plates and drank till their bill came.

Back at the hotel, they undressed in silence. Their room, cleared of the evidence of their passionate struggle, welcomed their unease without dispelling it. An angry David pondered Amélie's lovelessness, her frenzied respect for proprieties, while she mused sadly on the pertinence of the evening's events. It was their last night. And their future rendezvous, left to the whims of fate and desire, drew a swarm of question marks under their bed's canopy.

CHAPTER FOUR

*A*mélie was supposed to meet a friend at the Flore at half past twelve. Chantal was always late, but she did not mind waiting. She liked this café, the waiters' long aprons, the bewigged, sad-looking manager standing near the cashier's desk, and the regular customers, like the two old gentlemen seated on the imitation red leather banquette at the back, reading and making discreet comments on the press from behind newspapers spread out in front of their espressos.

They were always there. One wore a Swiss voile shirt with a dark, faded business suit: a handsome man betrayed by aging, whose cumbersome burly build contrasted with a bilious complexion; his austere, old-fashioned elegance breathed the bygone era of Central Europe. While his companion, a bald civil-servant type, his eyes magnified by the thick lenses of his glasses, had the rosy cheeks of a chitterlings sausage fancier, and wide suspenders on his round belly. Both of them sneaked away at the same time, just before the lunch crowd turned the pub's peaceful landscape topsy-turvy.

Twelve thirty-five: they got up. Amélie greeted them by a slight toss of her head. Were they brothers in arms, or retired office colleagues? At any rate they were dignified in their observance of a discipline known to them alone. It was also wise on their part to flee the crowd of press attachés in miniskirt business suits and the day's divas jostling one another at the narrow stands.

Her eyes swept the room, in search of a new center of interest. A muddy-complexioned young woman kept on scraping her spoon in her cup of coffee. Her pointy, fleshy breasts stood out, unbeknownst to her, like intriguing, bold stowaways. Amélie thought she recognized her bulging eyes, her energetic yet vulnerable features. An actress no doubt, whose careless attire, tentative demeanor, preserved her incognito. Shaped by the cool transience of the place, a mystery lingered above the tables of the café.

Chantal was running really late. Like a crossword-puzzle buff intent on solving a particularly thorny definition, Amélie concentrated on identifying this discreetly famous woman. Though history, or the workings of institutions, seemed unintelligible to her, Amélie was thoroughly adept at everything that dealt with the love affairs, disappointments, and irrational opinions of both large- and small-screen stars. She possessed a fund of information as vast and delicately shaded as the civil code, one systematically updated by magazine gossip columns, which furnished her with a subtle jurisprudence geared to uphold a point of tittle-tattle law.

Amélie would never admit to these little weaknesses. Recognizing celebrities became for her a special point of honor. She was peeved when she failed to do so. Over and above the fact that the bits of futile information cluttering her memory held no glamor in her estimation, she felt that behaving like a rubbernecker would only open a void between her and people of renown. She preferred to keep silent about her satisfaction in identifying a famous musical composition, or a painter's trademark brush stroke, as these did nothing more than produce proof of her limited culture.

She made do with the gaping holes in her education, as with her working-girl inquisitiveness, and Peeping Tom voyeurism. She kept them secret, beyond detection. Nothing made her more uneasy than the same vulgar traits in others. She squirmed when an acquaintance would exclaim: "Get a load of so-and-so!" or longed to disappear in a hole in the ground when someone declared with shameless self-satisfaction: "That's a Picasso!" These mediocrities compromised her reputation, tarnished it by association. Her carefully retouched image was bound to be destroyed.

Hidden behind a screen of impassibility, she was no longer concerned with the impression she was making; her silence in front of a painting could pass for the reserved qualification of a scholar; her placid demeanor in the presence of a person of mark might mean she did not know him, or failed to be impressed. This was her no-fail system. It did not hold anyone's attention, but Amélie accepted herself as she was, and in so doing safeguarded her pride.

She even managed to attribute to herself a role of some importance by modulating the nuances of her indifference.

Should a pretentious, arrogant leading lady enter the Flore, Amélie would punish her by not paying her the slightest attention. She derived satisfaction from sapping the woman's certainty of being admired. But should the diva be likable, Amélie's attitude altered imperceptibly: kindly disposed, she refrained from spying on her in order to preserve the star's precious incognito.

Whew! She'd figured out who that woman was. Didn't she play Anaïs Nin in that Henry Miller film? That's the one.

A deeply moving and comic actress with a rock crystal voice. Amélie was delighted to have detected a famous actress under such drab attire.

Suddenly, unexpectedly, Amélie felt like extending her wishes of success, and communicating her admiration for the actress's choice of roles and her interpretation. It was like a fever, leaving her aflutter. In her excitement she felt awkward, wondering whether the vanishing of all her principles might not be due to the actress's lack of notoriety. Could she have ever imagined that this outpouring of praise would not be met by weariness?

Her impulsive gesture was doubtlessly ridiculous. Nothing ventured, nothing gained. She could still draw back. Reviewing the various stages of the woman's career in order to bolster her speech, she selected words that expressed her thoughts: sincere, unaffected, flattering yet not fawning, reconciling warmth and concision by the judicious use of the right pitch.

When she thought she was ready, she analyzed the situation once more. The young woman was still alone; she wouldn't disturb her long. And were she forced to retreat before the actress's cold response, were her intervention to sink into ridicule, she was free to stammer and falter in her speech, since none of her acquaintances were there to witness her embarrassment. The time had come for her to react, or rather to take action. The woman seemed discouraged. Perhaps she had just been jilted, and would be only too happy to know she was appreciated. It was delightful after all to receive a compliment as delicately phrased as the one she had just prepared.

Like a schoolgirl ordered to the blackboard, Amélie gathered up her courage to walk over to the woman. The actress raised her eyes, putting on the ghost of a smile, as she listened to Amélie hastily delivering her compliment.

—Thank you very much, was all she said, pursing her lips to form a polite pout that clearly indicated she was concluding their conversation.

Back at her table, Amélie thought over the episode. Her blood had rushed to her head, throbbing in her temples. She felt the flush of her cheeks. But it was done! She savored for a few moments this victory over her natural reluctance, calmed down, yet realized she was disappointed. In spite of her well-meaning reserve, the actress did not seem to have been touched by her kindness, and her pertinent comments.

Perhaps it was the wrong moment? Perhaps there was no right moment to approach a person in public life?

She avoided letting her gaze drift in the direction of the actress's table, tried to think of something else. All of a sudden she was pierced by a shooting doubt: Didn't the actress she admired have an aquiline nose, finer features? A vague face, different from the one she approached, was emerging from her memory. Her head was swimming as she tried to separate in her mind one face from the other. Casting furtive glances at the woman, she urged herself to keep calm. Feverish and nauseous, she felt she must have made a mistake.

Then a vague recollection wormed its way through her discomfort: the woman facing her was also an actress. She had played in Louis Malle's latest film, belonged to the same age group as the other, and was equally talented. But what was the good of knowing this now? By complimenting the wrong person she had reached the zenith of greenhorn naïveté.

Overcome by embarrassment, Amélie clutched the edge of the table as patients grasp the arm rests of the dentist's chair. Only a bad moment to live through, she reasoned, trying to get out of this state of mind. The actress was paying her bill. She wouldn't see her again. Soon, this whole incident would be as forgotten as properly treated tooth decay.

Amélie waited for the young woman's departure to allow her muscles to relax. Relieved of the actress's gaze, she had to face her own. Theorizing about notoriety had always seemed to her innocuous, imaginative, reassuring; all she could see in it now was the manifestation of affectation and vanity. She felt as though she were inhaling the musty odor of a full ashtray after having smoked a cigarette and enjoyed the twirling smoke and the warmth of the paper cylinder between her fingers. She had to admit to herself that she had never left the flock of the faceless admirers of celebrities.

Chantal came bolting through the door fifteen minutes late, having double-parked. From her seat at their usual table she could keep an eye on the meter girls.

—Before anything else, I must tell you about my blunder, Amélie declared.

She turned her mishap into a side-splitting tale. Chantal roared with laughter. And Amélie, glib and mirthful, transcended her humiliation in the act of telling it.

Chantal was wearing one of those white silk blouses with a stock collar, signaling at a distance the sexlessness that was the ideological imperative of her American law office, which ensured her colleagues' vigilance in regard to the least show of femininity. Animated, as usual, she detailed for her friend the various aspects of the race she had to run in order to leave her office at the time their New York associates were waking up.

The two women ordered salads and coffee without a glance at the menu. They always took the same thing, as much for the comfort of a predictable routine as for any concern about diet.

Looking at her insipid salad, Amélie was amused by her absurd respect for conventions, which made her peck like a bird in Chantal's company, whereas with David, to avoid being dull as dishwater, she'd enthuse over the waiter's description of warm foie gras washed down by sauternes.

Should she tell Chantal about her adventure with David? Perhaps it was a good idea. Usually she confided in her husband when in need of advice or venting her spleen. Now that it was essential to hide from him all this baseness, she needed an accomplice. Chantal was no doubt gifted for keeping secrets and furnishing alibis. . . .

However, it seemed immodest to speak of the two men in her life to a friend who didn't even have one. Then again, did she really wish to allow Chantal, who thought a secret as painful as a splinter, into her confidence? She knew in advance that to conclude this transition in all fairness, she'd have to follow up with additional secrets accompanied by a reasonable portion of licentious details. . . . Better keep silent.

Chantal began with a description of last night's dinner party, all the time chewing disconsolately her lettuce leaves. A confirmed bachelor, she had left her car in the parking lot so as to reconcile the insecurity she felt in going out alone in the evening with the hope of meeting the man who, by driving her home, would transform her life.

She had gotten into the habit of calling the hostess to find out which of her guests would pick her up, and leave to fate her end-of-evening escort. Amélie had many doubts about the efficacy of this device, but, having met David in a gas station, she could not comment on statistical likelihoods.

The avowed aim of the dinner party was to introduce her to a loafer whose main attribute was his recent divorce. A single glance sufficed to reveal the incompatibility of their recipro-cal futures. She had had to endure the obligingness of the host-ess who, under the mask of good intentions, had orchestrated this introduction to rejuvenate the staleness of their social get-togethers.

—You know, Chantal said, voicing her indignation, these ladies all wear revealing, low-cut dresses aimed to arouse their dinner partners. I can't tell whether they mean business, or want to prove they're still fuckable and that their hubbies are off-limits.

—And, let me guess, after dinner, they park their hus-bands in a corner of the living room, with your intended, and whisk you off to the opposite side?

—Exactly! Chantal giggled. You should hear how they speak of their husbands! Listing in every detail their failings and weird habits.

—All the better to put you off, right?

Crush

Chantal ordered a pitcher of hot water to thin her espresso. Amélie had to have her sugar substitute. After which, making their way through the crowd to get their bill, they parted on the sidewalk.

Amélie ran to her car. She was as short of time as people are of money. So, a windfall set her off on greedy, totally unreal splurges. She was supposed to meet David at half past two, and get back to her office at four: just enough time to drop by the new art show at the Grand Palais.

All access to the Alexandre III bridge was closed to traffic by the presidential motorcade that smoothed the arrivals and departures of distinguished visitors invited to the Palais de l'Elysée. No turning back. She was stuck! There was nothing to do except grumble under her breath at the government's kowtowing to banana republics, and swear out of a spirit of solidarity with her confrères at the wheel. At this moment she felt more French than when casting her ballot in the polling booth. This sudden realization of her patriotic fervor filled her with stoic indifference to the postponement of her cultural escapade. As she watched the convoy's departure in the direction of the Ecole Militaire, she knew she'd be late for her tryst.

At David's she rang the intercom's buzzer. No answer, nothing. A scribbled message was fastened with Scotch tape to the entrance glass door: "For Amélie. One o'clock. My love, your secretary can't locate you. I'm stuck all afternoon. Call me in the office. I love you. David."

—Merde! she heard herself shout.

She went back to her car, slammed the door shut, lit a cigarette, brooding over her disappointment: She hadn't seen

David for ten days, ten days spent numbing her body, fossilizing it, so as not to feel his absence! Returned today from shooting a film in Alsace, he had arranged this rendezvous. Her belly craved him. What kind of game was he playing?

She was getting mad. David had no idea of the stunts she performed to get free. What hadn't she invented to come to him? A plausible business appointment, for her staff; an editorial committee meeting where she would be unreachable by phone, for Paul's sake. She had made a big dent in her credit with her daughters by telling them she'd come home too late to kiss them good-night. And all that for nothing! And to think of the intricate arrangements she'd have to make to see him again. Did he really wish to marry her, as he claimed? How could he hope to convince her of it if he failed to make himself more available?

She regained some of her cool after listing her grievances. She was perfectly unfair. David was in love; it was he who was running into her parsimonious time allotment, her reluctance to plan the future. There were times when she saw herself as a vampire, quenching with him her boundless sexual thirst while infusing his being with frustrations.

She told him she was not about to exchange a husband overwhelmed with work, a settled family life, for another busy man who had not sired her children. But if she sought shelter behind this carefully wrought case, which appeared rooted in common sense, the real reason was her grudge at his failure to convince her of dropping everything to live with him, of not being irresistible enough to silence her scruples.

Her introspection was getting too serious. Amélie decided to stop this barren self-absorption. Now she had the time to go to the art show, and to the movies. After all, David was entitled to his thwarting impediments. Life was full of un-predictable happenings, which ought not to unleash paranoia attacks!

She was suddenly ashamed of loving him so badly, and felt the need to make up with him though she alone experienced their falling-out. She knew the address, if not the telephone number, of David's office. He was rarely there, spending most of his time home or outside on the shoots. She decided to call on him.

The entrance to the building on rue François Ier must have been elegantly old-fashioned before the glass partitions and the potted plants. A receptionist, involved in refreshing her nail polish, seemed to have collapsed inside her booth.

—David M., please? Amélie ventured, taken somewhat aback by the woman's lowered face.

—Got an appointment? she inquired without look-ing up.

—Sure thing, answered Amélie, ironically concise in the hope of getting a reaction.

—Second door to your left, beyond the stairs, was the roguishly curt answer.

Amélie, expecting to be announced, had no desire to in-trude upon David at the wrong time. She made her way along the corridor without the least bit of wholeheartedness, full of doubt as to the wisdom of an unexpected visit. She knocked on his office door so timidly that she was forced to repeat this operation a number of times before she was heard.

—Come in! David thundered, annoyed with the minc-ing ways of the pusillanimous person behind the door: Amélie! he claimed, as she entered.

—Am I disturbing you? she inquired tensely.

—Of course not, my love. Come in and sit down.

He looked at his watch, adding:

—I've got all the time in the world. My next appointment is in three-quarters of an hour. What a lovely surprise! It's so good to see you!

Amélie recovered slowly from what she feared would be considered a lack of tact. She told him of her desire to see him, and forgetting his telephone number.

—I had forgotten how beautiful you are! David interrupted her.

Amélie smiled with satisfaction, pleased with her judicious selection of a pleated skirt, when she realized she might have been locked in David's arms for the past five minutes. He hadn't made a single move, too busy suggesting that he show her the final draft of the poster for his new film.

—Where did I put it? Oh, yes, I know, he muttered.

He circled his desk, went over to the closet, whose sliding panels were covered by mirrors. Amélie followed him with her eyes.

His grey suit enveloped him in seriousness. He spoke of his movie as though he wanted to lend a professional character to their reunion, one in harmony with the décor. Seized with the desire to rid him of his constrained attitude, Amélie had stopped listening. She was going to get back at him for the ease with which he reestablished his self-control the moment he left the bedroom.

She got up, feigning interest in the poster, and put her hand on the fold of his fly. David grew still, questioned her with his eyes. Amélie put on a candid air:

—Your health is my only concern, my love. I'm checking out your vigor.

She clasped the contours of his penis with her fingers, stroking it to assess its hardness, fingers on the prowl for any positive feedback. David scolded her, amused, yet upset at the prospect of his imminent meeting.

—Now look what you've done! I've got a hard-on. Amélie, you are impossible!

Fueled by David's scrupulousness, the incongruity of their surroundings, the possible interruption by a secretary, Amélie acted as if her blind gropings were far from responsible for the bulge threatening to burst the seam of his crotch:

—But darling, I must check this out . . .

Kneeling, she spanned the broadness of his erection with her mouth, shooting warm puffs of breath through half-opened lips along the length of his cock encased in gray twill, as if practising scales on a mouth-organ. A suddenly silent David abandoned all resistance before Amélie's lack of faith. Obviously, she needed to feel in order to believe.

Leading David to the edge of his desk, she propped him up facing the mirrors, presenting her provocative ass by leaning forward to pursue her delectable investigations. David relished both the impunity of contemplating Amélie riveted to his prick, and the surge of power derived from seeing her down on her knees, at work on his cock. He lolled back, watching her unbuckle his belt, pulling down the zipper of his fly.

Amélie took her time freeing David's cock from its white cotton prison, extricating it with joyful pleasure, rubbing it with conscientious concern so as to dispel any cramps inflicted by an awkward position. Only then did she dip charitable fingers into the tight fit of his underwear, seeking to comfort his balls after their prolonged isolation. David was already breathing heavily. Amélie lowered his underwear over his thighs, staring hungrily at his thickened prick.

He moaned with impatience. Affecting an indifference she was far from feeling, Amélie knelt below the cock prodding at her forehead. She tasted the flavor of his balls, gathering them into her mouth with her lips, counteracting the hindrance of his underwear to explore the hidden folds of his flesh with the tip of her tongue. There she lingered, in the dark nook under his balls where his dick took root, fondling the secret recesses of his groin.

When David felt her tongue glide upstream to his cock's peak, he took a deep breath, hoping to store up self-control before she could engulf him in the sweet torture of her mouth and play havoc with his increasing excitement. He allowed himself a break, letting his eyes roam. Catching his own reflection in the mirror, buttressed against the desk by Amélie's mouth, he watched her straining ass force her skirt to the top of her black stockings.

—Pull up your skirt! he panted.

Amélie seized the sides of her skirt with her fingers, bringing it above her waist. Her panties had indiscreetly slipped into the clef of her buttocks, clinging to the wetness of her pussy.

—Take off your panties! he ordered.

Amélie lowered them promptly, making a show of stroking her ass. She opened her thighs, letting him glimpse the moistness trickling from her throbbing cunt.

Inspired by her provocation, David grabbed his dick, shoving his pelvis toward her like an imperious toreador defying a brave bull.

—Say you love my cock! he commanded.

—Yes, it's beautiful, big and hard, said Amélie, wetting her greedy lips with her tongue, eyes widened by lust.

David savored Amélie's subordination, her enticing vulnerability, and the sight of her rounded thighs nipped in by the tourniquet of her lowered panties.

—Tell me you want to suck me, he went on.

—Oh, yes I do! Give it to me, she begged eagerly, deeply aroused by his hoarse voice and curt orders. It made her shiver with masochistic submissiveness, assigning her a role as sweet as it was painless.

—Here! Take it! he demanded, his stern disdain adding spice to this delectable exercise.

She proceeded. Propelling her tongue orbit-like around his prick as though licking her chops, she gluttonously lapped up the drops oozing from the furrow of his glans. Narrowing her lips, she suckled at the crown of his cock, tonguing the ridge etched down its length.

—Yes, that's right, suck me hard, David spurred her on, lurching into her mouth, his hands flat on her head, sustaining and prolonging Amélie's voluptuous inspiration.

Amélie impaled herself onto David's stiff rod, retracting his foreskin with her fleshy lips. Guiding his length down her gullet, she squeezed him between sucked-in cheeks, licking the tip of his prick wedged against her palate. Then she drew back, smoothing out the loose tunic of flesh wrinkle by wrinkle while she fingered the weight of his balls, rolling them in her hand as if testing them.

—Oh, that's so good . . . You're a real fine little tart . . . Go on! gasped David.

With her tongue, Amélie took the pulse of David's desire, adapting her pace to the reflexes of his penis. When his large balls grew suddenly compact under her fingers, she glanced up. Countering his sudden dizziness, David firmly grasped the sides of the desk. He let out a yell, his knees buckling. She felt the spasms of his cock in her mouth, the spurting of his cum down her throat.

She sucked him tenderly holding his hand, waiting for the troublesome vulnerability of his uncontrollable emotions to subside. Then like a drinker after downing a foamy pint of beer, she wiped her lips with the back of her hand.

—You killed me! he groaned, reeling.

—My poor darling, whispered a falsely compassionate Amélie. You have exactly two minutes before your next appointment. I'm leaving now.

She pulled up panties and stockings, with the quick precision of one who, although aflutter, never lost her faculties. She looked at David, haggard, his trousers bunched about his ankles, and her own detachment struck her as a triumphant, heady whiff of freedom, a new independence defying her addiction to David. She added before leaving:

—No hard feelings, I hope, my angel? Call me.

She headed toward the door; David stopped her:

—Amélie . . . I love you.

She turned around as she was about to cross the threshold of his office. She smiled at him. Light-headed and stated, she savored the taste of his semen lingering in her mouth. Outside, it was a beautiful day.

CHAPTER FIVE

—You must be kidding, you're
not serious, are you? was Amélie's response to David's telephone call at her office announcing the following news:

—No . . . yes . . . well . . . I'm moving next week.

It was quite unexpected. David had spoken to her of the
house at Saint-Germain-en-Laye he had bought for his family. It remained empty after the departure for Morocco of his
former wife and son. He used to say he'd sell it, and now he
was moving in!

—You'll see, it's a beautiful house . . .

He went on praising his property with all the smooth
sales talk of a real estate broker, listing the various advantages
of suburban existence, particularly west of Paris, with its spa-
cious houses and conveniently close shopping malls.

Amélie couldn't help spotting the clichés in his chaff as
if she were drawing up a detailed inventory. Her own fierce-

ness troubled her. She saw herself as a once-domesticated hunting dog, returned to its true nature. Was she disappointed? With David living outside of Paris, they'd see each other less frequently. Or was she vexed not to have been consulted? Cutting remarks were clogging the back of her throat. She kept herself from voicing them, back pedaling so as to reestablish a climate of loving goodwill.

After all, she reasoned, David was entitled to a change of opinion, to living where he saw fit. They had made no plans for a life together. In that house he probably felt at home. Perhaps he wanted to change his lifestyle. He surely was going to explain, displaying a touching sincerity.

But David persisted, enumerating the positive aspects of suburban living: the elimination of the exorbitant rent on his Paris apartment, the excellent railway network and highway system between the capital and the outlying districts. He assured her of his neighbors' good manners, not sparing her a single trivial detail.

His vocabulary was as poetic as an administrative report. Amélie felt like the echo chamber for a lexicon of tedious terminology. David, she decided, was not about to say anything more because he had nothing to say. This vulgar street-hawker patter took the place of inspiration.

She kept silent. Her irresolution was suspended between disbelief and amazement, as though above a badminton net. What good would it do to express it? The only result would be a series of misunderstandings. David would attribute her hostility to his decision to move, not to the pitiful reasons he gave for it. She'd fly into a temper. They'd quarrel. Her wise and cowardly silence struck the right note: that of a discreet compromise.

—You'll still come to see me? he inquired anxiously.

—Of course, my love. Perhaps a little less frequently, but I'll find a way . . . I'll manage to do so.

Amélie hung up. She sat immobile at her desk, stiff with wary anticipation, like a patient expecting to feel the cold smoothness of a steel stethoscope. She could feel herself opening the door of the room in which she kept her feelings for David. A musty smell mixed with the odor of moth balls hovered over the slip-covered furniture, filling her with dread. She quickly moved away.

*D*avid put down the receiver with a sigh of relief. The hardest part was over. He had told her his intentions. She could have put him back in his place, bombarded him with questions, or reproached him for his decision. But she had said nothing, even though, in his desire to make her understand, he had never stopped talking. The essential lay in the answer she'd given him. She would come.

How could he explain to her the conflicting, passionate connection he had to the house in Saint-Germain-en-Laye? It was much like the bond between a son and a possessive mother. He had admired this house when he was a penniless immigrant. To have been able finally to afford it was his victory. It lasted only a short while. Paris, he came to realize, was more elegant, more trendy. Everyone told him so as soon as his first films became hits. He moved after his divorce.

Then Amélie appeared. He started dreaming of a future. How could he, camping out in a studio on the Right Bank, expect her to leave a conjugal home? Were she to do so, it would be the rash act of an unthinking person, and she certainly was no idiot.

No sooner had he considered selling his house than he felt stripped of his good luck, as though he had lost a fragment of his foundation. He felt a nomad again, limping through life. Amélie seemed out of reach. She never spoke much of her husband, who appeared to be pressed for time and engrossed in his work. Hadn't she felt abandoned, having to bring up her daughters alone, sleep in an empty bed, go out to dinner by herself? Most certainly. Otherwise she would never have looked at him twice. He could never have seduced her.

The house had a large garden, made for laughter and children. The owner of such a house could be a suitor. There he'd be sure of himself, able to convert her to a peaceful kind of happiness. Now that he had completed his film, he was free for a time of any obligations, and would go out as little as possible. She could count on him to be available at any moment. She'd notice how serious and loyal he was, and in the long run he'd win out. He was tenacious, and determined to be patient.

$\mathcal{A}$ few days later, the alarm clock rang at seven. Amélie was alone in her bed. Awakened by a fit of insomnia, Paul must have been in the living room for many hours. But Amélie's difficult awakenings did not dispose her to conjugal benevolence: she realized she was irritated by the thought that her husband was expecting her to prepare his breakfast, instead of satisfying himself the demands of his appetite. She went to the kitchen, heated the coffee, toasted bread, and took the tray into the living room.

Crush

—Thank you, dear, Paul said absentmindedly from behind his newspaper.

The girls were still asleep. Amélie threw a toilet kit, big as a new born babe, into her bag, and drew her bath. Let's see, she said to herself: what's today's tall tale? Oh, yes, an obligation in a provincial city! She was going to spend the night at Saint-Germain-en-Laye. David had just moved in. She was curious to get to know his house.

Stretched out like a hammock suspended between two trees, the nape of her neck resting on the bathtub's edge, the tips of her toes upon the enamel, Amélie was amazed at her calm; and yet it was exciting to vanish for a day from the account books of her organized existence! She was free. She could have driven to the coast, caught the first plane leaving Roissy, gone to the movies or the antique shops . . .

Staring ahead, she left her body and mind in her bath's warm water, grown milky from the piece of soap slipped out of her fingers. The sight of her creased fingers, like those of a drowned woman, brought her back to consciousness. David was expecting her. She had lingered much too long. Her comatose dream state affected her like an intake of fresh country air, which suddenly makes the city atmosphere unbreathable: her double life revealed itself as one more obligation.

This is normal, she said to herself, in search of reassurance. Her profligacy had deprived her of all lightness of being as day after day, since she'd met David, she raced through all her activities. No time for the hairdresser, lunch with girlfriends, or relaxed conversations with writers. She had to organize things in order to be free for a long lunch or manage the traditional five-to-seven slot. Setting up each rendezvous demanded such effort that she ran her feet off organizing them, never once questioning what she was doing, or allowing her desires to ripen. No wonder her lust for fantasy still thrived, she concluded.

She felt faint as she stepped out of her bath on faltering legs, her face beaded with sweat. "That bath was too hot!" she said to herself, as if to avoid answering the question spread out upon the bathroom walls. Was she pursuing this affair because of love or lust, or had the obstacles along the way made a liaison, reinforced by habit and cowardice, more appealing?

Once in her car, Amélie feigned good spirits so as to experience a measure of optimism. She felt she fully deserved the right to enjoy the day, having gone to such trouble to entrust her daughters to friends and to organize Paul's evening.

She avoided the banks of the Seine in order to meander through the streets till she reached the *périphérique,* the beltway around the city. She got lost in the maze of access routes to the highway. Feeling dizzy, she drove round the traffic circles that had replaced former crossroads. Finally, on the *route nationale,* she struggled to differentiate between various commercial centers, attempting to follow David's directions.

Amélie was lost in a Bermuda triangle of neon signs: carpet dealers, leather merchants, sportswear shops, and factory outlets; all seemed dangerously similar. Sweating profusely, led astray by the slapdash, repetitive architecture of garishly-colored warehouses, she held on for dear life to the succinct itinerary David had scribbled for conscience' sake only, since for him the trip held no hardship. Finally she recognized the sign of the do-it-yourself shop, which announced the end of her troubles.

She slowed down upon approaching the pebble-covered drive. Her car's wheels crushed the neatly arranged stones with a crunching noise that sounded like the comforting promise of a rich, well-kept family estate.

David's house was not the awful villa she had expected. It was much in the style of Frank Lloyd Wright's architecture: two storeys without frills, pebble-dash, or climbing ivy. There were large bay windows, cement walls, a love of light and design.

A spruced-up Amélie stepped out of her car. David had taste. This subversive building, standing amid aggressively pretty whereabouts, was proof positive of it. He greeted her with a grandfatherly chaste kiss.

—Let me show you the place.

Together, they walked through the reception rooms stretching out between glass and brick. Amélie applauded, pleased with the simplicity of the design, which reminded her of an unfinished garment's tacking. To think she had lived in fear of exposed beams, and tapestry snakes placed at the bottom of every door to keep out the drafts!

She kicked off her shoes, feeling the flat coolness of travertine tiles. David's furniture looked elegant, even precious in this simple décor. Everything was dust-free, enameled.

—Where are the boxes? she inquired.

—The boxes? David sounded surprised.

—The movers' boxes! I expected to unpack, put away . . . I thought we'd hang paintings, picnic on the floor. You've been here for only three days, and one would think you've lived here for the past ten years.

David was blushing with pleasure.

—Quick work, right? I didn't want to greet you in a house turned topsy-turvy. I wanted everything neat, impeccable. I wasn't about to make you work, when we have so little time together.

Amélie kept silent so as not to deny the disbelief full of admiration, the dazzled astonishment David assumed to have detected in her voice. Actually she felt no such emotion. She had traveled to his house in order to roll up her sleeves and set the place to rights, looking forward to wild outbursts of laughter, and a healthy stiffness due to the strain of physical labor. This could have been a welcome hiatus in their erotic transports.

The whole subject of housework was a contentious one. Early on, Amélie had confessed to performing domestic tasks with neither savoir faire nor a taste for it. She had also asked David to expurgate from his conversation all practical considerations, acting as an invalid who feels his aches increasing twofold at the slightest mention of his suffering. Actually, it was a delicate way of asking him to avoid a subject he found to his liking.

Thus David, always thoughtful, got into the habit of taking care of everything when they were together.

—Leave it alone, I'll take care of it, he'd say, as soon as she made a move to peel a potato, wash a dish.

It lasted only a short while. Pretending to forget that she knew how to cook, vacuum, or even drive in a nail, he would assume the role of a victim:

—All right! I'll make dinner, he'd snort, balking at this chore.

Yet, he wouldn't let Amélie perform any task.

—Leave it to me, he'd insist in a peevish tone, as soon as she tried to lend a hand, whisking away the frying pan or the dish rag.

Nor could she ignore or remain indifferent to his required service. David in the kitchen, David cleaning house, expected Amélie's compliments. Such was the present state of affairs. Forced to listen to the exegesis of domestic labor, and the running commentaries of David's talent and kindness, Amélie had given up on all her obligations.

*O*nce again David had demonstrated his good intentions. Once again she was at the end of her patience. But wasn't she overestimating her enthusiasm for manual labor? Why did she feel so disappointed and angry?

Soon she realized she had put herself through a workout, like an athlete getting ready for a championship event. Fearful of hating every instant of this day, she had pumped herself up, exalting the good-humored simple pleasures she'd savor with David, the harmonious turn in their relationship. Having forced herself to put her best foot forward, she pinned her faith to the spontaneous character of this sentiment.

Without acknowledging it, she had intended to purchase for herself a line of conduct. She'd have turned this move into a dream of unison and gaiety. Charmed, David couldn't have failed to stay madly in love. Now, with this program change, she had to improvise. Deprived of the boost in energy she would have experienced during these domestic tasks, she was not certain she could rise to the occasion.

David interrupted her musing:

—Come, he said.

The command rustled with echoes of David's erotic in-structions. Amélie was filled with sudden desire. To state it point-blank during this solemn visit was too risky. A disguised, treacherous attack would be better strategy. She had to make him want her.

Concerned with Amélie's reactions, David had gone to a lot of trouble in order to create an excellent first impression. All traces of his marriage, of his past in the house, had been carefully eliminated. He had taken down the draperies with the floral print beloved by his wife, and ordered a Scotch plaid instead. He moved heaven and earth to have these curtains delivered before his move.

The wall-to-wall rug had been changed. He had cleaned the closets of old bobby pins, half-empty face-cream jars, an odd shoe here and there. These objects, abandoned by a wife eager to leave the place, had vanished as if they had never been. Doubting his good taste, growing anxious, he had studied every detail of his house, presenting it and himself like a suitor, wearing his butter-colored leather gloves on the day of proposal.

She showed her enthusiasm by being talkative. David began to relax. Determined to take her on the complete tour of the house, he savored her amazement, as well as every one of her comments. Faking an impulsive interest in the second floor, Amélie walked up the stairs ahead of him. She quickly climbed the first steps, stopped as though waiting politely for him, actually hoping he'd notice her dress, made see-through by the backlighting of the window on the landing. He was eye level with her buttocks.

Crush

She was wearing a short, sleeveless dress, held closed by a great big bow on the back. The numerous openings were so many avenues of approach to her lithesome body. David tried not to stare at the contour of her hips, seen like shadow play through the light material of her dress. He'd had a hard-on since she arrived, as soon as she had stepped out of her car. But he wanted to exercise self-control in order to establish a solid basis for their conjugal plans. Were he to jump her at every turn, she'd take him for a satyr.

Amélie sashayed up the stairs. Hypnotized by her ass, obsessed by the memory of her skin as smooth and soft as the finest leather, David could no longer control himself. He slipped his hand between her thighs. She was hot, open, horny.

David lifted the sides of her dress and plunged his head in the direction of his hands. His face sheltered by the airy fabric in a siesta penumbra, he recognized, nesting round her vulva, her odor of freshly baked bread. Under the lampshade of her skirt, Amélie's ass, magnified like the detail of a painting, obscured the perspective. Her skin, iridescent like an earth-baked ceramic amphora, met his eyes. It was smooth, fleshy, vigorous, under its pale, celadon-hued glaze, which betrayed the boldness and unseemliness of her nudity.

David's vision blurred. He groped across the checkerboard relief of light and shadow. Some obscure islets remained to be discovered, deflowered: the top of her thighs, like a cloudy sky sheltered by her ass, the camera obscura between her legs.

He pursued the crown line of her panties, traced the contours of her buttocks with saliva, before skimming along her slit. Amélie moaned, reeled. David held her up by her hips:

—Turn.

He removed her panties, pulled up her dress, made her stretch out on the steps. Kneeling, he observed her cunt with a surgeon's gravity. Then, lapping the down that hemmed her glossy, purple vulva, he moved down to capture her clitoris between his lips.

Amélie braced herself, let out a cry. She was going to come too soon, without having seen his face, his cock. Catching her breath, she said:

—I don't want to come without seeing your hard prick. Show me how much you want me.

David emerged from Amélie's cunt, his eyes feverish, his lips shining and wet. He carried her off into the bedroom, placed her upon the bed. Standing next to her, he unbuckled his belt, opened his trousers upon a triumphant prick, whose tip glowed with impatience. Amélie tried to draw close, but he stopped her with a gesture. She raised her eyebrows, seeking an explanation, then, giving in to the straining nerves and muscles between her thighs, she turned her head to watch his reactions while she slowly finger-fucked herself.

Without uttering a word, he held up his rod, alternating a fast to-and-fro motion with ample, measured gestures. Seeing him masturbate himself in this fashion, Amélie felt she was stepping beyond the threshold of intimacy, transgressing the limits of discretion. Embarrassed by his masterful technique, the expertise of his own fingers upon his cock, she had the impression of spying on a male fantasy, as though she were watching this scene through a keyhole. She stroked her pussy faster.

Breathless, she gave full vent to her boldness. It was exciting to arouse David's helpless panting at a distance, using only the lightest touch of her fingertips upon herself, to see his

forehead bead with sweat, witness the spectacle of solitary pleasure staged on the border between shame and obscenity. Before crying out and letting herself climax, she directed her gaze
straight into David's eyes, as though to warn him.

David held back his orgasm. He watched Amélie's hand
contract convulsively, fall upon her vagina. Only the whites
of her eyes showed as she drowned in a tidal wave of sexual
bliss. He moved forward. She was still limp when he turned
her over on her belly. Firmly grasping her hips he raised her
rump and took her as he stood by the edge of the bed.

Unbearable, indestructible, David's desire for her bor-
dered on insanity. Amélie's body, her skin, her ass obscured
his work, his dreams, his priorities; they had become an obsession. Condemned to the irresistible pull of her slit, he sank
into it as though falling into an abyss. He burrowed himself
into her furiously, seized by the spasmodic throbbing of
her cunt.

Amélie felt David take her brutally. Interpreting this
assault as a homage, she enclosed him tightly within her, ready
to savor his eruption. But he was hurting her, pounding away
at her as though moved by rage, by unexpressed desire so overwhelming that they made him forget to take or give pleasure.
Used in this fashion, she had no need of seeing his face to know
he had drifted far away.

He suddenly came to his senses. Amélie's inert, resigned
body offered no resistance. He curbed his violence, modulated
the powerful strokes of his loins. He felt tired, crestfallen. He
laid Amélie down, kissed the back of her neck. She remained
docile, immobile. Her woeful smile filled him with terror. He
stroked her cheek. He could so easily lose her if he went on
loving her with the demented passion of a convict on the loose.

—Marry me, I can't live without you.

—I'm already married, she said.

—I don't give a damn; I'll convince you; I'll wait as long as I'll have to.

He fell asleep. Amélie carefully freed herself from the tangled sheets and proceeded to make her way in the direction of the bathroom whose door, swollen by humidity, was hard to keep shut. Once there, she let a thin stream of water run into the tub so as not to wake David up. There was an unpleasant hothouse smell in the room. She slipped on a peignoir and was getting ready to return to the bedroom when she noticed the shower stall. It appeared to screen a dressing-room.

She rushed inside. The room, lighted by a night-light, seemed to be a storeroom promoted to the rank of walk-in closet. The elegant cupboards within smelled of cedar and fine workmanship. Curious to check them out, Amélie opened them one by one.

It took her a while to fathom the function of the letters and numbers inscribed upon the edge of every shelf, deduce the classification that she gropingly reconstituted. The numbers went from left to right in horizontal order within each closet, and referred to the garment's color: white shirts in tray number one, yellow in two, and so on, from light to dark.

A shirt she pulled out from a center pile, checking it as one might a test tube, revealed the number of its attribution sewn on the back of the collar, as mothers do when packing their children off to summer camp. Amélie tried to push back in her mind the growing uneasiness she felt. So compulsive, and not a whit of space for a garment other than his own! How did his ex-wife manage? However, she pursued her detective work, deciphering the more subjective and delicate typology of the letters. The vertical classification referred to the nature of the garment: *A* for formal shirts, *B* for blazer shirts to be worn with an ascot, *C* for sports shirts . . .

—What are you doing? David asked. He was standing framed by the shower door.

Amélie gave a start:

—You scared me!

Caught in the act like some pitiful whippersnapper. To avoid looking embarrassed or, worse still, admit to the hold he had on her, she put on a defiant, alluring act.

—I admire your sense of order. You'd make a great butler.

—Is it supposed to be a compliment?

—Don't be mad, my love. You know what a mess I am . . . So, obviously . . . you impress me as an extraterrestrial being.

—Well, what's so extraordinary? I've been doing this for years, now that I can afford a cleaning woman! They do it all wrong, put things away haphazardly, without rhyme or reason!

David's explanation sounded rational. He showed himself to be a practical, rational human being. Keeping track in this fashion helped avoid the disappearance of warm socks and gloves, all these winter things one looks for in vain when packing for a skiing vacation. How well she knew the anguish of last-minute searches. His system was undoubtedly a precious time–saver.

Methodical, organized, he was in the right. This was undoubtedly the best way of controlling reality. To deny the importance of everyday life, as she arrogantly persisted in doing, made no sense at all. She had acted foolishly, and now no idea what to do to be forgiven.

—I love you.

—Too bad! he answered.

Hearing these words, Amélie's goodwill and repentance faded. She took a look at David. He was not angry. Then why did he make use of antagonism as a stylistic device? She saw no advantage in it. Was he trying to hide his embarrassment, his inability to react with simplicity and kindness to a show of affection, or was it simply a device to mask the fact that he had nothing to say? She changed the subject:

—My love, I'm famished . . . And I haven't yet seen your kitchen.

—You're hungry? I'm going to make lunch, he stated in the weary tone of a happy man burdened with new responsibilities.

He took her by the hand, led her to the ground floor. The kitchen's decoration was helter-skelter: walls covered by a patchwork of grey and green tiles, selected at various times by various owners. Formica furniture clashed with traditional, potbellied sideboards.

David declared he'd now devote himself to the art of cooking. This restaurant-keeper jargon was his way of dismissing with a joke a hobby he enjoyed. Amélie sat down to watch him, her elbows upon the oilcloth table cover. He cooked as he made love. Competent, experienced, he mused on what he wanted, took his time to make sure he was in prime condition. Then, all at once, bursting with strongly focused inventiveness, he'd combine bold, unusual flavors.

She watched him chop up herbs, handle the blade of a knife as he sliced a piece of meat, one hand flat on blood-glutted flesh. She kept a close watch on every gesture, seeing him knead, mince, stud the fat with cloves. She was fascinated by his skillfulness, nimble fingers, intimate connection to matter. He kept a running commentary on what he was about to perform, as articulate in this context as he was about sex. He could speak for hours of fricassée, rabbit stew, the difference between round steak sirloin and veal gristle!

Flabbergasted by the wealth of his gastronomical vocabulary, Amélie asked many questions. He emphasized esoteric words, scanning them like some culinary incantation; then he grew quiet, too absorbed to talk. With his eyes on the pans, mouth gaping with expectation, lips swollen with desire, he didn't even see her. She, however, kept on goading and circling him, determined not to be ignored.

—Smells wonderful! Could I have a taste?

—Come on! It's not ready yet! he scolded her, smiling with pleasure at her impatience.

Amélie had just finished setting the dining room table when David appeared, a napkin draped over his forearm. He pushed open the swinging door with his foot to bring in a steaming dish. A happy expression on his face, he awaited the first mouthfuls, Amélie's first compliments. She tasted, marveled, offered her congratulations. Next she tried to converse.

—It needs salt, don't you think? David interrupted her. Is the meat cooked enough?

Amélie's silence, broken by exclamations, reassured him. If this was the price to be paid for a successful lunch . . . so be it. She was willing to put up with this exchange of onomatopoeias.

Following the meal, a walk in the garden. Made self-conscious by this green square, Amélie felt awkward, clumsy.

"Nature, what's the good of it?" she had often wondered. It gave her no energy, no joy. What's more she seemed to be the only one of her kind. On the rare occasions when she admitted to these feelings, people voiced their amazement, doubt, and disapproval.

And yet that's how it was. She wilted under rain, burned in the sun, like a hothouse plant. One of her outdoors activities was to rise above these petty annoyances. The other was to memorize the scenery.

The sea reminded her of a mottled cashmere sweater. The reddish tint of the soil of Provence was like the rouille of bouillabaisse. Looking at the roots of olive trees, hanging from the hillsides, she was reminded of the torsos of black men, their frizzy body hair woven together like thickets. Embarrassed by the incongruity of these metaphors, Amélie would censor herself. Was she deprived of poetic sensibility, had she no culture whatsoever?

She'd stare at the horizon, in search of honorable references; gape at an empty beach, to find the contrasting stretches of sand of a Tanguy painting. She pursued Cézanne's palette in the rocks, and Vermeer's pale yellow in her florist's jonquils.

She sought to forget her coarse first impressions by dint of a quest for refinement. However, she grew rapidly winded. Her undertaking would then appear to her as artificial, ridiculous. Her mind rejected these affectations as cultured poses. Piqued by the uselessness of lifting these tenuous scraps of culture, she renounced paltry attempts at appropriating bits of scenery, making up her mind to submit, without stepping back, to the elements' supremacy.

In David's garden Amélie became bookish. Like a conscientious student using a yellow marker to underline a text's important sentences, she made a mental note of broad, burly trees, bushes spreading like gigantic escaroles, broomlike spiny shrubs.

She shepherded her memories of various gardens: Villandry, Vaux-le-Vicomte, her grandmother's vegetable patch, wondered about aromatic gardens, which reminded her that she had probably never completed her reading of *A rebours*. But these vague references did not help her to have a clear notion of David's garden, to express a sensible point of view.

She ventured an awkward compliment: The garden had an almost Japanese kind of rigor. After one complete lap, all Amélie could smell was the odor of new-cut grass, all she felt was overwhelming boredom. David led her toward a lean-to backed against the house.

—I've got to trim some shrubs. You don't mind, do you?

Obviously, David was counting on her for a bit of conversation. A distrustful Amélie sat down carefully upon a veritable rug of clover and thistles, as scrubby as her door-mat. She had to admit she had nothing to say.

Her mind dimmed by watching the insects around her, curtailed by an itch brought on by contact with the grass, she was incapable of the merry, witty bubbling he had expected.

Not wishing to denigrate his recipe for ordinary happiness, she tried a peaceful half-smile appropriate to the silent lethargy of well-being. She was playing for time.

When could she possibly leave without hurting his feelings? Once inside the house, what the devil could she do? Stupidly she had not packed any books. She missed her daughters. She couldn't do any of the things one does at home on days of leisure: file papers, paste photos in albums.

She missed the anonymity of the Paris apartment that sheltered their rendezvous in an atmosphere free of other associations. There David proved to be impulsive, unpredictable, insatiable. Here he was gardening, fixing the house, and planning their future. He seemed different when he was himself. He assumed she'd bloom. She was bored out of her skull.

Inside the house she vacillated between relief and frustration. To want to give David the slip was hardly a cause to rejoice. Actually pulling it off, with such indifference, would not bring happiness, either. Where would it get her? Free to come and go, she was nevertheless under house arrest.

Four o'clock. Her idleness allowed her to gauge the weight of her discomfort. Pregnant with their six-month-long complicity, this divergence struck her as a miscarriage.

Deeply depressed, she had to fill the void. Vertigo would yield to sensations. There had to be biscuits or cocktail snacks in the kitchen cupboard. A hurried, nervous search for a substance that would cram her stomach revealed a box of cookies. She opened it feverishly, unmindful of the brand, the expiration date.

With the cookies in her mouth, she stopped thinking. Her jaws seemed to wreak their vengeance by crushing the shortbread dough. She was instantly comforted as her mouth, flowing with saliva, acquired a lining of warm pap, as soothing as a poultice. Within her sated body, matter had dispelled the anxiety of the void. There went the whole box! Amélie left the kitchen feeling bloated, nauseated. She went upstairs, where she remembered seeing a TV.

Arranged in alphabetical order, the videocassettes rested on ugly metallic shelves like parts of an Erector set. Having painfully decoded the VCR directions, Amélie curled up in a great big armchair to watch Abel Gance's *Napoléon*. That should fill a bit of time.

The emperor was dying in a smoke-filled room when David let out a yell from downstairs.

—Amélie, where are you?

—Up here! Watching television.

—My love, I'm so sorry. I forgot all about what time it was. I saw the light failing . . . I looked at my watch . . . It's horribly late.

—You must have trimmed all the trees of your garden, didn't you? Amélie shouted back, putting on a playful tone.

—Far from it! Branch by branch, it takes a while. I'll continue tomorrow. But you must be hungry.

—Not really, she answered in a sluggish voice.

Her answer did not mean anything. She might have had a bit of appetite, or been starving without admitting it. She could also have lost her spirits. Actually, the thought of food made her nauseous after her cookie orgy and sedentary afternoon. But she had no substitute activity to suggest. It was the first time in David's company that she reasoned as a traveler lost in a region devoid of tourist attractions. She was in need of a visitors' office to assist her in this place without movie theaters, museums, restaurants, a place that left her devoid of all desires. Her imagination had run dry.

Beset by bizarre ideas, she thought of playing parlor games, which she detested. Then she invented unexpected impediments, like looking at a movie with David. She took exception to making love again, since using sex as a pastime seemed particularly repulsive.

Peeved by her own utter absence of initiative, she followed him to the kitchen. Moving step by step through his reasonable, well-ordered existence would make her burst inward with boredom and bitterness. She was bound to leave him if she couldn't alter the present state of affairs.

Dinner was silent, since she failed to chatter. David seemed pleased with his evening. He expressed the desire to retire early, drawing the curtains, closing all the doors, even those of the bedroom and bathroom. Then he promptly fell asleep.

Her eyes wide open in the dark, Amélie dwelled on her malaise. At home, she was in control of the semidarkness, leaving doors half-open to let in a bit of light. She had always been afraid of the dark, as well as fragmented spaces, closed doors and shutters, drawn curtains. Besides, David's rigidity before falling asleep, like that of a praying bigot, turned her off. He must have been going over his duties as a man of property: Was the alarm on, as well as the automatic sprinkling system, and the gas flow? He had to check in his mind that he had not neglected any of the above.

She remembered her boarding school, the dormitory's deceitful quiet, which misled the housemother. There were a few students like her, for whom breaking with the strict discipline of the institution was a form of artistic endeavor.

These associations of ideas were profoundly disturbing. She had to admit to herself that, lying by his side, she felt like shouting, dancing, indulging in the worst of pranks.

David's breathing grew heavy, regular. She got out of the bed surreptitiously. Since she had had no part of dinner, she was hungry. She opened the bedroom door all at once, preventing the hinges from creaking, made her way down the dark stairway, and filched in the kitchen a bag of potato chips, which had escaped her afternoon raid.

Her excursion lacked grandeur. She fought against its mediocrity by returning to the second floor. She imagined herself in flight from Sodom, with Lot, her husband. And if David were to discover her in the middle of the night, stealthily climbing the stairs in defiance of divine interdict, her fingers clenching a bag of chips, she would turn to a pillar of salt. She stopped, confounded each time the wooden steps creaked, and assumed a tragic pose in the silence that followed.

Having reached the landing, she congratulated herself upon her performance, decreed she had done her best, like the bicycle racer at the end of the Tour de France. To go back to bed seemed ridiculous after this epic effort. She locked herself up in the television room, felt her way in search of an undiscoverable light switch. Finally she gave up and, trusting her memory, walked in the direction of the set. Seated in the lotus position, the screen her only source of light, she crunched her potato chips noisily. This is a form of enjoyable mischief, she reflected, regretting the absence of fellow viewers whose bitter protests would meet her noisy interruptions. Having made up her mind to watch as many programs as she could endure, she waited for exhaustion to set in before joining David in bed.

CHAPTER SIX

*B*arely six o'clock; Amélie's work was interrupted by a profound silence, as disturbing as a mysterious presence. It was an unusual silence, which seemed to have invaded the press office suddenly. How silly of me! Amélie told herself. It was an evening of general exodus at the start of a long weekend. She left her office. The car radio crackled warnings about driving conditions and road safety. This was of no concern to her. With Paul in the United States and her daughters in the country, there was no need to hurry. She had plenty of time to call David to let him know she was alone this weekend.

Her apartment seemed somehow larger, more fluid, because those who lived there were absent. She listened to music, watched *The Blues Brothers* for the tenth time, and realized she had no desire to see David. However, she decided to call him for conscience's sake, much as one inquires about the health and state of mind of a child gone to summer camp. She waited until midnight, the hour when her husband usually fell asleep, and cautiously muffled her voice as though she were not alone:

—Did I wake you up?

—No.

His concise answer and categorical tone sounded hostile. She reasoned with herself. Why should he resent a furtive night call, a secret from her husband? She thought he judged her severely because she was passing judgment on herself, guilty of lies that rendered David's accusations meaningless. Anxious to redirect the conversation, she asked:

—Where are you?

—In bed. And you?

—In the bathroom, she answered, reclining on her bed.

—What are you wearing? No, don't tell me . . . I loathe the idea of you in bed with him . . .

—You don't think that I wear see-through negligees for my husband, do you?

There was nothing he could do—Amélie's voice always gave him a hard-on. He had expected her call all day, had not stepped out of the house. Beset by mental snapshots of her body, he strung them together in his mind, like drawings for an animated cartoon, and now his head was bursting with cumbersome fantasies.

—What are you doing? Are you seated or squatting? He decided to make love to her by phone, moving each provocative word forward, like pawns on a chessboard.

She laughed, not quite sure of herself. What was he after? Dirty talk? He didn't wait for her answer.

—Your throaty laugh is making me hard.

About to indulge in a conversation bound to unleash desire, Amélie experienced the heaviness of a deadlock. Yet, already excited, she dared to go on:

—Is that so? Touch your prick. Tell me if it's hard.

She strained her ears to listen to David's hand run down his belly, imagining his stiff, plump penis slowly expanding to its full stoutness. She heard his breathing and the crumpling of the sheets. David let her direct him, his cock sheathed by her raw words, by her embarrassment, which was leaking out through her audaciousness. He continued:

—It's thick, hard. I'd like you to suck me. You'd like that, wouldn't you?

—Oh, yes, she sighed.

David was aroused by her assent. He thought of the words he might have extracted from her, were he able to touch her: how she longed to suck him off, swallow his cum. He'd have put her on all fours, called her a whore while shoving his penis deep into her mouth. He began to masturbate, his fingers tightly closed about his prick, his thumb curled toward the inside of his thighs to caress his balls:

—Tell me if you're wet.

Amélie dipped her index finger into her slit, exploring the source of the dewy wetness irrigating her vulva. Her fingers frolicked and fribbled in it like vacationers on a deceptively quiet shore:

—You're getting me all excited . . . I'm dripping wet . . . D'you hear me touch myself? . . . I close my eyes, imagine I'm sitting on your cock . . . Gently because it's so big. I suck it up into my cunt . . . I hold your balls between my buttocks . . . I'm masturbating . . . You're watching me do it, you feel me flow all over you . . .

Amélie was a beginner in this kind of audacity. She got caught at her own game. Aimed at exciting David, selected with an alchemist's infernal skill, the words she uttered, rising like potent exhalations from the devil's own alembics, sent their fumes up to her brain. Her cheeks aflame, her cunt replete and swollen with desire, she plunged her fingers into the moist interior of her slit before harrying the ruby-colored cap on her labia's crest.

David listened to the flow of Amélie's words, as provocative as a striptease, yet they spawned fantasies more potent than the most shameless baring of flesh. Unpredictable, and as effective as the numbers of a safe-deposit box, they shaped a frenzied combination, accelerated the motion of his hand upon his prick, propelled him to uncover the tip of his glans:

—You're going to make me come too fast . . . Play with yourself . . . You'll let me suck you, won't you? I'll stick my finger up your asshole at the same time. You like that, don't you?

David's words became images. Amélie could see herself legs spread above his mouth, coming down upon his lips, her loins arched to welcome his finger. She could feel him suck her clitoris, penetrate her ass . . . Her fingers became whirling dervishes spinning in an ecstatic trance.

Judging by the whirring over the telephone, Amélie could no longer control herself. David envisioned her teetering on the edge of orgasm. He could not hold out any longer. To make her come now, he upped the ante of obscenity.

—And my prick in your ass, you like that, don't you?

Amélie was overcome by a succession of blended images. David was about to sodomize her. On all fours, trembling with apprehension and expectation, she spread her ass to him.

Caught in the trap of his own imagination, David clearly saw her proffered asshole, her submissive hips. His prick pointed at its target, he prepared a strategic move whereby he'd approach her cunt only to fuck her in a surprise attack. His balls were full, swollen. He was about to shoot his load.

—You're coming? he asked hopefully.

Amélie heard herself utter a primitive moan, which rose from her gut like bile. David's discreet groan echoed back to her like a canon song.

—I've got it all over me, he complained at the sight of his sperm spread upon his belly.

Emerging from orgasm, Amélie was astonished, as she always was, by the way her shuddering cunt took possession of her entire body before beating a hasty retreat.

—That was so good! she moaned.

—You're going to sleep soundly.

—Oh, yes, she answered smiling.

She put down the receiver.

The following day, after a night peopled by nightmares, Amélie was awakened by the calm of an empty apartment. The pulsation of her arteries, pounding the silence like a metronome, dictated a measure of gravity. David had become an obsession. The memory of their conversation of the previous night, the violence of her orgasm, pressed on her temples like a hangover. At the core of these contrasting feelings, a diffuse, opaque bad conscience was beginning to rise. She had to make sense of it all.

Gradually, Amélie had begun to feel she was slipping toward sham. At first she had curtailed her meetings with

David, to disguise her boredom, much as one edits out a film's slow scenes. Then spreading their encounters thin, she made up all kinds of obstacles in order not to see him. She could no longer pretend being quietly happy, feeling that it would be like dreaming in front of a perfumer's display window, its fake scent-bottles filled with colored water.

She could still feel the gusts of the boredom she'd experienced during her visits to Saint-Germain-en-Laye. Seated in an armchair next to the sofa in which an expansive David poured his heart out to her, exhausted by her day at the office followed by bottlenecks at the Paris exits, she could feel her eyes close with boredom. She recalled watching the level of wine in David's glass as he sipped it after dinner. How long would it take him to drain it to the last drop, getting ready to go to bed? She was bitterly disappointed when he poured out another, absorbed by the charms of his own conversation.

Occasionally, when she was tired or short of time, David would meet her in Paris, at a Porte Maillot or la Défense hotel . . . The desk clerk registered no emotion. The room fridge opened on generically labeled shelves: sodas, plain mineral water, chocolate . . . You had to pay to open them, to look. Once out of every two tries, it didn't work, like defective automatic distributors in deserted train stations. Nothing to be done!

Their encounters followed an immutable scenario. She could reconstitute every scene. No sooner had they entered the room than David showed himself cold, distant, almost unpleasant. He didn't take her in his arms, showed no joy in seeing her. Walking around the bed, whose size alone revealed the function of this anonymous room, he'd go over to the only armchair, settling in it ostensibly to distance himself from the role of stereotypical lover that she attributed to him.

She'd pretend not to notice his lack of tenderness, his bad humor. She'd begun to understand his reticence in her presence, the overwhelming resentment, the flood of reproaches he held in check.

When he was home alone, comforted by the sound of her voice on the telephone, the prospect of an imminent meeting, he was able to fool himself: traces of her presence, memories she left in the house took the place of her company. He preferred this kind of life to losing her. But he gauged his physical need of her as soon as, reaching out, he could touch her. In retrospect, he felt robbed, abandoned.

Stretched out upon the bed she would chat to entertain him, to avoid apologizing for their shaky liaison. Time enough to smoke one or two cigarettes. David would get up from the chair and pace the room throwing burning glances at her. Yielding to his desires like an addict unable to shake his habit, he'd ask her in an expressionless voice to undress, stroke him, suck him off.

His lovemaking was frenzied. He savored the orgasms he inflicted on her like a punishment, himself on the verge of fainting. In the silence that followed, pleasure acquired the seriousness of a death sentence, confirming their dependence on one another.

She had to leave. David apologized for having spoiled their meeting. The knowledge of being deprived of her presence prevented him from savoring the joy of being with her, whereas the memory of the moments spent together conferred on him the strength to endure without her.

Ready to go, her bag over her shoulder, she listened to David enumerating his apprehensions. His moping was bound to become tiring. She reassured him, speaking slowly so as not to show him that she was in a hurry.

On the point of leaving her, David would grow suspicious. She didn't love him as before, he was certain of it. Having run out of reassuring phrases, she'd start laughing, but an uneasy feeling crept into her being, that of having misplaced the certainty of her love while making provisions to preserve it.

David lacked an inventive imagination, a lightness of the spirit. She made him unhappy. She should have let go, retreated, left him. But she also cared for him. In order not to jump at the chance of a breakup, which David's uneven temper offered her, she had padded their love story with cheerfulness and spontaneity. She had actually reinvented it.

For his sake, she conversed with passion. She combed her past in search of childhood memories and family tales, painted amusing portraits of her relatives. Her capital of recollections, emotions, anecdotes was lavishly spent. Sold out of stock, she was concerned she'd stop pleasing him were she unable to deliver a parcel of new ideas, like an arrival of early fresh vegetables. She set out on a quest of new inspiration to surprise and entertain him.

She bent her mind to greater vigilance, sharpened her eye, her judgment, as to books she was reading, paintings she looked at, phrases overheard, making it a point of honor not to serve him bad imitations, clichés, as though the unreasonable demands she made of herself in this regard were a form of compensation for her miserly commitment to David.

Talkative without being a chatterbox, she allowed David his monologues. When he was through, she formulated her discoveries, using the lightest brush strokes, as though they had just grazed her conscious mind.

David never answered her. She didn't resent it right away. Perhaps she had overdone refinement to the point of incomprehensibility. She was accustomed to this situation. When she heard someone interrupt a remarkable paper, she kept quiet in the illusory hope that the tiresome pest might be won over to the cause of silence. Her subtle disapproval and annoyance seemed to her sufficiently explicit. She sent this message with conviction, but no one ever heard it.

In the long run, she understood that David didn't listen. He loved the energy she expended on conversation, her gestures, the movement of her lips, her glowing cheeks. When he felt she was moved or sprightly, he'd interrupt her to tell her he desired her. He smiled at the music of her words, convinced it was the proof of how happy he made her. She didn't get discouraged. Touched by David's credulity, the faith he had in her happiness, she was sparing of her remarks, distilling a scanty portion of her chatter at each of their encounters. She tried countering his seriousness by arranging all manner of surprises. She hid her love letters to him inside his car, small gifts in the house, in a bag of coffee, or the bathroom cabinet.

She'd invite a tailor to his house when he needed a new suit, or leave her home at dawn, or in the middle of the night, to bring a kiss to Saint-Germain-en-Laye while her husband was sound asleep.

Their affair had the illusory cheerfulness of a conversation dotted with funny stories, yet taking a perplexing turn between two puns.

Sometimes she'd relax, weary of her premeditated inventiveness. It was tiring to always show enthusiasm, or organize the unexpected. But her liveliness collapsed like an under-cooked soufflé when she faced David's grandiloquent decla-rations of love or his fits of despair. Yet still she'd felt an obligation to dust off their ennui, as though it were her re-sponsibility to improve their daily life.

Their liaison was nearing its end. Instead of coming to terms with it, she resorted to therapeutic obstinacy. She applied gaiety like a balm upon the whole stretch of their meetings. She kept on deceiving herself with these successive distractions, alternating treatments and dosages.

By refusing to acknowledge she was making alterations to their affair's story, treating it like a badly cut garment, she wouldn't admit it was she who botched the pattern. She was always evasive, to avoid being at the mercy of her feelings. She wouldn't give their liaison the slightest chance to acquire sub-stance. Wallowing in David's foibles, she questioned his intel-ligence, his propensity to really listen. Mortally afraid of becoming the slave of her desires, she had failed to voice them. Sidetracking the issue by the offer of a sham exchange, she managed to keep aloof.

In a way it was a master stroke. David shared with her idyllic moments, but he did not know her. He believed her to be whimsical and vulnerable, tried to reassure her by lavish-ing declarations of love, sound advice, and offers of money, were she short of it.

He had no idea of what he had to give: his body and the way he dwelled in it. Humbly trustful in regard to sensations, David made of his flesh his soul's lining, his fervor's tool. He had no clear notion of his talents, but he taught her abandon. Reborn from his desire to pleasure her, she slipped into her own body as into a new garment.

For David, who refused to believe she wouldn't divorce, despite her categorical nays, their differences seemed of no consequence. Yet it was upsetting.

She couldn't lie to herself, or dream of living with him after their Moroccan escapade. But she hadn't yet reached the hoped-for state of apathy or detachment. Trapped by her affection, she kept on accumulating memorable moments spent together, so that time had conferred upon their affair the fullness she feared. She no longer knew whether she could exist without this amorous fiction, rooted in her flesh, in every one of her reflexes.

She wondered what it would be like to live without him. Assessing days filled with thoughts of David, weeks illuminated by the beacons of their meetings, their conversations, she experienced a retiree's disorientation. What would she do without this double life, its constant hurry, anxiety, pressure? She'd have to get used to the forgotten rhythm of tranquility and routine. Resuming a simple existence was a terrifying prospect, a void that one associates with taking up golf.

Like the clerk casting a final glance upon his desk, his check-room hook, Amélie surveyed the presently useless tools of her affair: the safe-deposit box in the bank for his letters and the extravagant pieces of jewelry he had given her; the direct telephone line to her office, reserved for him alone; and all the memories accumulated in her mind, where they would surface from now on, grinning like an old hag.

To break with him would lead to silence, as surely as death does. In the days following their separation, there would still be some milestones along the road. David saw his son every second Saturday, visited his barber on rue du Faubourg Saint-Honoré, and he was planning a holiday in Sardinia after the Venice Mostra. It wasn't possible to numb people before leaving them, so as to catch up with them in one's thoughts, or require letters, friendly meetings, if you wished to be forgotten. David would alter his habits, get a new phone number. He'd move. Lost forever. How could she face never to hear again the voice of a man she confided in every day?

Amélie kept for the end the most shameful of all her thoughts, much as a hostess does when she places the least brilliant of her visitors at the end of the table, in the hope that the rigor of protocol would serve to mitigate the guest's mediocrity: Would she still feel beautiful without David, who couldn't conceive of her falling asleep without having reached orgasm, any more than he believed a man could remain indifferent to her ass, her voice? How could she get along without his stubborn desire, immediately detected by other men who followed her as dogs sniff a bitch in heat.

CHAPTER SEVEN

*A*mélie had not yet reached a decision, but she was relieved at the thought that a veil had been lifted off ideas relegated to a corner of her conscience, which plagued her like a persistent stitch in her side. She got dressed quickly.

Saturday was chores day: bills, social security forms, telephone calls . . . The pace set on those days was that of a treasure hunt. Checkbook in hand, Amélie followed an itinerary whose logic she alone could fathom, including the stops along the way in the paper-cluttered zones of her apartment.

She walked over to the fireplace, where still-unpaid bills were resting in a prominent position, retrieved her mail between the kitchen toaster and the breakfast baguette, and, crouching under the living room table, went through papers piled helter-skelter in an attempt to convey to her husband the illusory impression of orderliness.

The telephone answering machine was her journey's important port of call, with its memory joggers, and intrusive messages accompanied by incomprehensible names and telephone numbers. She found her notes, cockled and wet, at the bottom of a puddle, utterly illegible. Her ceiling, with its humid corona, dripped like a nose afflicted by a winter catarrh. It was the kind of bothersome occurrence, devoid of panache and significance, that nevertheless inflicts its pressures, much as a bureau chief coerces his personnel into submitting to his pettiness.

Annoyed, she made a mental list of the round of cares awaiting her attention. The floor above her apartment was made up of fifteen maids' rooms. With her paltry sense of direction, and complete ignorance of plumbing, she felt incapable of locating the source of this leakage.

Ten in the morning on a Saturday. The tenants must have gone out. She couldn't count on the concierge, busy with house-cleaning jobs in the neighborhood to make ends meet.

Driven to some kind of action, she stepped out on the landing. The back stairs, reflecting the style of the service quarters of a previous era, were putty-colored and egg-shell white. Amélie climbed the narrow staircase, hemmed in by heavily painted walls.

Judging by the presence of a toilet on the landing, the dimly lit hallway could lead only to makeshift hovels. She felt sorry for those living there but preferred these simple maids' rooms to the fake renovations made by professional decorators: stucco moldings, mausoleum-like marble, the wooden panels inspired by Swedish saunas.

Nor did she rejoice in the so-called improvements in her neighborhood: modest cafés turned overnight into garishly neon-lighted, bay-windowed Tex-Mex establishments; the new bakeries' displays of breakfast rolls, jelly doughnuts, and chocolate Danish presented on tablets framed by gilded brass fixtures, as though this daily fare were rare pieces of jewelry.

Lured by gospel music, so out of place in such a French corridor, she set out on her inspection tour. She had to knock on the door repeatedly before getting a response.

—Just a minute! shouted an angry male voice.

The man who opened the door had a telephone propped by his head in the hollow of his shoulder. He had hastily girded his loins with a bath sheet.

Disconcerted, Amélie feared the badly secured towel might fall, putting her in an even more embarrassing situation than the present one. Definitely ungracious, he raised his eyes and chin in a mute address signifying "What's it about?"

Amélie stammered:

—Am I disturbing you? I'm your neighbor from below. There's a leak in my apartment . . .

—I'll call you back, he growled into the phone, with a curtness clearly directed at Amélie.

She was always thrown by aggressiveness. She remained speechless. After hanging up, he merely tossed out in her direction:

—Yes?

She could feel herself blush. She didn't know where to begin, how to explain her problem to this man who didn't seem inclined to help her, particularly since he most probably had nothing to do with the flood in her place. Bewildered, she stared at him: tall, slender, beardless, he looked like a movie romantic lead.

The cad was interrupted by the light-switch timer, which plunged the corridor in darkness. Seeing her standing at his doorstep, looking lost in the dark, he softened his tone:

—Please come in.

His studio was a good size, obviously carved from two or three maids' rooms. He introduced himself:

—Serge Munz. I'm an oaf. Sorry.

Amélie introduced herself. She resumed her tale of woe calmly. He was examining her offhandedly, but his look made her self-conscious. She shifted her weight from one foot to the other, encumbered by her arms like a gawky adolescent. The music stopped. They were both taken aback by the sudden silence that threaded its way between them, revealing their separateness. They had nothing in common, except the music. It had held them briefly, as though caught in gelatin.

All of a sudden Serge desired this distant stranger. She froze. It happened in a fraction of a second. Serge fantasized about holding her in his arms. Amélie thought of running from this indecent tête-à-tête.

From the next room one could hear running water. Serge turned his head in that direction, on the lookout, as though hearing with his eyes.

—Merde! my bath!

He dashed, flinging a door open:

—Oh, no! Merde!

Amélie heard him sloshing through water, turning off creaky, rusty faucets. A mean, triumphant smile appeared on her face. She was pleased that the situation had reversed itself, even more than in having solved the enigma of the water damage. Embarrassment and unease were about to shift camp. Her presence in this man's apartment had become legitimate. Thanks to this discovery, she felt confident, on top of the situation. She drew closer.

Moving on all fours, Serge Munz was busy mopping the floor with a piece of sacking. Dripping with perspiration, he didn't cut a fine figure. She took in this scene, feasting on it like a boa ingesting its prey. Then sated, she inquired magnanimously:

—Can I help?

—You don't think that on top of it all I'll ask you to mop my bathroom! Sit down and I'll be right there . . .

Amélie surveyed the whole room. This was the right moment to satisfy her curiosity, awakened by this peculiar man in his forties, a kind of eternal student, eternally broke, elegant in demeanor but with unpleasant manners.

She saw he was a kind of collector. The walls of his room were covered with shelves crowded with brightly colored plastic figurines, giveaway toys from McDonald's meals. The ubiquitous Mickey Mouse came in all sizes and forms: watches, telephones, alarm clocks. There were lead cartoon characters from *Tintin, Spirou,* and *Blake and Mortimer*. Obviously he had not grown into adulthood. His rumpled bed, covered with a feather comforter rolled up in a ball, suggested fitful sleep or messy habits. A couple of books, dramatic texts, were scattered on the night table.

Serge materialized by Amélie's side:

—Well, one thing is certain. I'm the guilty party. What are we going to do now?

—I have no idea, answered Amélie.

They burst out laughing. Serge suggested:

—What if I were to make amends by taking you out? It's close to lunch time . . . I'm starving.

—Me too, Amélie answered, realizing she hadn't had anything to eat all day. She added: It's only eleven-thirty . . .

—We don't give a damn, do we?

*T*he weather was cold and dry. The oblique rays of the sun fashioned in the asphalt a dazzling anthracite trail, like a mountain slope. Amélie smiled, fascinated by this mirage of altitude created by the reverberation.

A fatalist and a shirker, she welcomed an unexpected holiday from responsibility. Since she couldn't contact her insurance company before the weekend ran out, why not forget the tedious chores of Saturday and leave the rest to destiny?

Serge was watching her from the corner of his eye. He liked tall, cold, haughty women. She wasn't his type. But she was pert, attractive despite her shortness and transparent skin, which revealed an alluring network of veins.

She winced when, going up rue de Tournon, Serge stopped in front of the Chinese restaurant where David frequently took her. The door was open, the place empty: not a single waiter. All the tables were available, none seemed desirable. They shilly-shallied before deciding to call on someone. The echo of their hesitation rebounded off the bistro's walls, like a bat's sonar, returning to their ears without having been stopped by the obstacle of any company.

They finally sat down for fear of showing a ludicrous irresolution. No sooner done than they regretted their choice, as though, yielding to a headwaiter's impatience, they had ordered an unwanted special of the day. Pretending to be satisfied, they started an innocuous conversation to avoid losing face, as the Chinese would say.

Timidly, they applied themselves to becoming acquainted. The restaurant owner, a fat Chinese matron, stepped out of the kitchen to greet with deference the day's first clients. Her reserved attitude in regard to Amélie was unusual. Surprised to see her with a man other than David, she pretended not to recognize her.

Usually, after shaking hands, she would launch into a description of how hard it was for her to stick to a diet, since she'd yield in the middle of the night to irresistible desires for vanilla ice cream. Imitating her accent, Amélie gave Serge a sample of the discourse he wouldn't hear now that he was with her. He laughed.

"Here I go again!" she thought. "First I make him laugh, and in five minutes I'll be flirting!"

Subject to fits of despondency, Amélie tried hard to introduce gaiety into her life. She methodically cultivated her *joie de vivre* so as not to sink into despair. She joked with shopkeepers, smiled at strangers who whistled as she passed, held conversations with train-conductors, waiters, and old ladies sitting on public benches. The world then became as safe as a village square where one can mollify a cop to avoid paying a ticket, or elicit a smile from the postal clerk.

Seduction was a reflex she couldn't drop. Bitter experience taught her that most of her interlocutors would prove disappointing. She never derived as much fun from their company as from her pleasure in charming them.

A curious mixture of vanity and lack of self-confidence propelled her to act this way. Far from underrating the people she met, she conferred upon them qualities she'd been seeking for a long time before giving up hope of finding them. But she had doubts about her own worth, taking the initiative of gaiety to avoid facing the indifference she assumed she would arouse.

"There are limits to everything," she thought. After all, she wasn't doomed to seducing a neighbor responsible for flooding her apartment. He might possibly be able to engineer a fun lunch without doing the work for him. "Too bad if he turns out to be a bore," she reflected. She could always cut the lunch short.

So when he said: Tell me about yourself, it was the perfect opportunity to drop her flirtatious attitude. Like giving up smoking, it had to be cut short at once. With him she'd practice being insignificant. At least, she wouldn't waste her time. She had the impression of granting an interview to a reporter of the yellow press.

She weighed every word, delivered the official version of her life, keeping a strict watch over herself so as to avoid sallies or any witty remarks. She pretended all was divulged in the strictest confidence, as she piled one platitude upon the next. At last, pleased with her performance, she fell silent, careful not to restart the conversation and see what would happen next.

There was an embarrassing silence broken by the entrance of the waiter bearing imperial pâtés and a plate of steamed dim sum. Amélie had to bite her lips to stop herself from laughing. Ceremoniously, she applied herself to steady the mint and fried egg roll resting upon the ridge of a lettuce leaf. A perplexed Serge Munz gave the void a searching look. She was having a wonderful time.

—It's good, isn't it? he ventured as a last resort.

—Yes, was her answer.

She was delighted at the spareness of their exchange.

The restaurant was filling up. Most of the tables were taken. Serge Munz was silently chewing his food. Amélie realized that, in his company, she didn't fret over running into an acquaintance. They were too obviously bored with one another for their tête-à-tête to be compromising.

They were like those couples who, when eating out, never open their mouths except to ingest food. She always watched them from the corner of her eye, certain they took advantage of a heedless moment to secretly exchange a sentence on the sly, like naughty schoolchildren awaiting their chance to indulge in a bit of clowning.

Serge was about to say something when Amélie caught sight of David coming in. He was in the company of a young man, undoubtedly his son. He didn't seem to notice her presence.

—What's the matter? Serge inquired, seeing her grow pale.

—I've got a problem, she said in a whisper.

—What problem?

Amélie thought it over. She was supposed to be spending the weekend in Paris with Paul. . . . Had David ever seen her husband? No . . . Their paths had not crossed, and when David asked to see photographs of her daughters, she carefully removed those with Paul in them. So, this Serge Munz would do fine. . . . So far, so good . . . Of course, when David would catch sight of her, he'd realize how disturbed she was. . . . A normal reaction when you are peacefully ensconced in a restaurant with your husband, and your lover makes an unexpected appearance. Whew! All that was left to do was to transform into a husband the clod sitting before her.

Serge was furious. Not only was Amélie a self-satisfied bore, but she expected him to show interest in her little problems. And when, to be polite, he feigned concern, she couldn't even be bothered to answer him.

Amélie looked at Serge. He looked like a man at the end of his rope: jutting jaw, flaring nostrils, eyes shining with a metallic glow. He was about to raise his voice. She had to cajole him at once so as to avoid a scandal she couldn't pass off as a family quarrel. No time to finesse.

—My lover has just come in. I told him that there was no way I could see him, since I was with my husband.

—Well! That's some mix-up!

—Let me explain . . . Amélie went on. What I'm asking you is simple. I'd like you to behave as though you were my husband.

—A while back you certainly produced an expurgated version of your love life! Serge was enjoying his irony.

—A while back I had no reason to tell you about my romantic complications. I hardly know you. Beside, "a while back" I was playing the dope.

—What do you mean?

—I was trying to be as dim-witted and boring as possible.

She gave Serge, overcome with a fit of uncontrollable laughter, a sharp dressing-down, explaining how indelicate it would be to convey the impression of conjugal closeness.

— Amélie, you're delightful! Fine, make use of me as a husband.

David noticed them. He was surprised to feel an intense annoyance. Hadn't he come to this restaurant sniffing Amélie's trail, hoping to find her odor between these walls? He hadn't expected to discover her in an intimate tête-à-tête with her husband. Up to now, relegated to a parenthetical existence in Amélie's stories, that man had no definition beyond that of his function: a father role, the title of spouse, in short an abstract, variable, slightly bothersome presence. There he was in the flesh, inexplicably familiar-looking, endowed with substance like the jinni of Aladdin's lamp, but, unlike that supernatural being, unpleasantly menacing. Moreover, he was handsome. Looking him over, he wanted to bash his head in.

Amélie had an odd look. His arrival in the restaurant must have shaken her up. However, he wasn't up to empathizing with her. She was having lunch with her husband within the sanctuary of their illicit meetings, shamelessly undermining the magic of this place. Her unconcern offended him, filled him with doubt: Were Amélie and her husband having fun before his arrival?

Serge asked for the bill. Amélie was pondering the kind of look she ought to throw in David's direction before exiting. It had to be discreet, without seeming furtive, tender yet not saturated with love, since she was contemplating breaking off.

—Don't worry, Serge told her, noticing how tense she looked. You're merely leaving a bistro with your husband.

—All right, she sighed.

They got up to leave. David looked at them with a defiant air, and a shade of irony that made her uncomfortable. She returned his look, her eyes conveying contradictory emotions. Her only hope was that he'd select the one he needed.

Serge and Amélie walked off in the direction of their apartment building. Bothered by David's hostility, she kept silent.

Serge observed her closely. Her confusion aroused him, awakening fantasies of caresses stolen with impunity, as though from a defenseless sot. He envisioned a tactical movement whereby he'd seduce her by keeping her off guard. Then he pulled himself together, ashamed of this questionable thrill, not unlike that of a pervert taking advantage of the rush hour to feel up a subway passenger. Taking leave of her, he tried to be unambiguously affable.

—Don't hesitate to call on me. I can play your husband anytime. After all, I'm an actor.

—Really? Thank you. I'll call you next week about the leak . . . , she answered absentmindedly with a worried look.

CHAPTER EIGHT

*A*t the end of the meal, David and his son parted company. David walked away from the restaurant, obsessed by the image of his mistress's conjugal life. Then he had a vision of himself, ambling aimlessly, all alone. He felt excluded, rejected; he took pity on himself.

He had another look at the portrait he was painting in his mind, retouched to make it even more desolate. It was the sketch of a pale, poignant man, back bent, fully deserving of pity. It lasted only one moment. He stopped short when he realized he was aping sadness. What did he need this pathetic attitude for? In no way did this pretentiousness soften his confusion. It only made him ridiculous.

Back home, he walked through the house in search of projects, longings. He recalled his plan to wax the small stand in the living room, to weed his garden. But despite these good intentions, every object of his daily life seemed slip-covered. He remained aloof, indifferent, as detached as an abstentionist on election night.

—Let's look at things squarely, he told himself. His discomfort was as tenacious as sticky paper. There was no setting it aside.

Running into Amélie had proved unsettling. However, no important event had occurred. Amélie's family status had been established from the start. There was no reason to grow disheartened on account of the scene he had witnessed. As to the choice of a restaurant, he didn't hold exclusive rights to all the bistros of the rue de Tournon!

—A cup of coffee, a good cigar, and it'll be water under the bridge, he told himself, settling down to examine a pile of scenarios.

Far be it from him to let a crush crush him.

*A*mélie pulled her door shut, and sank into the living room sofa. Her affair with David had run aground, beached like some flummoxed whale. "It's the end," people say at the bedside of the dying. Had they reached this point?

—Darn! she exclaimed, trying to shake off her austere lucidity.

In the meanwhile, by running with the hare and hunting with the hounds, she behaved like a real bitch. She had no idea what to do next. Should she apologize to David, explain her embarrassment, or keep her cool as if nothing were the matter? She might make use of this chance incident to convince him that, under the circumstances, she had managed as best she could. To rush to the phone would only lend a melodramatic overtone to this episode. She'd call later that evening. . . . She had the whole afternoon to arrive at a decision.

$\mathcal{D}$avid found it hard to concentrate on his reading: the story of a minor government administrator in love with a dishonest civil servant working under her. It would have to be resolved in the space of ninety minutes, scheduled for the 20:50 slot on channel 2. Nothing to get elated about, but it was high time to get back to work.

Who'd be good for the role of the female administrator? Why not Marlène Daillant? She hadn't been in movies for a long time, and would no doubt accept the offer of a telefilm assignment. For the male lead, someone unknown would do. He reached for his directory of actors and musicians. Unconsulted for the past two years, it was out of date. No matter! He might at least get an idea.

He began to leaf through the dramatic-artist category, under *M* for men. The order was alphabetical. David lingered on every page, looking over calling cards illustrated by photos. There were profile and three-quarter views, but most of the actors were full face, their heads slightly inclined as though questioning him.

Some of these candidates were chatty, eager to convince. They spelled out their professional experience: such and such a drama school . . . films directed by . . . a vita in due form, complete with a list of available foreign languages (foreign accents if necessary), sports, acrobatics, pantomime; driver's license. Some declared their willingness to act in commercials. Others (famous actors or timid beginners) simply listed their names, that of their agent, an address and telephone number.

Serge Munz was one of the latter. His face under the letter *M* pierced David like the blade of a knife. A deep, unexpected gash opened in his being, exceeding anything associated with the consciousness of pain. Nor did he realize at once that he had suffered a mortal wound. He forced himself to go back to the photo, examine it again, the better to feel the oozing of the cut. He grasped the phone, dialed a number. The agency was closed. The answering machine advised: If you can't get through, try 01-12-00-32.

—Hello! The person in charge assured David that he did not disturb him in the least. It was a pleasure to speak to a man whose films he admired. A ninety-minute for channel 2? He could certainly help. . . . Mr. Munz? Very good choice, a pro. Handsome without being a lover-type, charming but not a charmer. He had a lot of success with women . . . perfect for the part. Oh, you want to think things over? As you wish. At any rate, he would be available if David wanted to pursue matters further.

David put down the receiver. So this was the man Amélie had had lunch with: a miserable actor without talent or reputation. "He must be her lover," he concluded, boiling with rage. And this idea, once expressed, astounded him.

—Her lover, he said out loud, as though testing a film's dialogue to make sure it sounded right.

The utterances he produced began to acquire meaning. They possessed an autonomous existence seeking its base of support in his memory. "He must be her lover," which explains why she hadn't mentioned his existence, whereas she enjoyed describing her circle of friends.

This line of reasoning bounced off the partitions enclosing his mind. David remained unconvinced. Amélie knew lots of people she never mentioned. This fellow might be some kind of cousin, a pal of her husband . . . It didn't mean anything.

Anesthetized by this confusion, David began to hope again. But a fusillade of questions assailed him soon: Why had she lied to him? Would she have mentioned a family lunch if she planned to join a simple acquaintance? And then there was her obvious discomfort when they happened to run into each other. And her conjugal lunch scene?

There was only one coherent explanation: This fellow was her *lover*. David immersed himself in the substance of this word, filled himself with its meaning, its import and consequence. He was trapped in the net of images he had woven: Amélie making love with Serge under his very eyes. Her undulating image became blurred, rose like a vapor as he tried to approach it. In her place he found a cold, dangerous stranger, unleashing within him a tumult of feelings.

—But why? he roared. The sound of his own voice frightened him.

𝒯he ring of the telephone startled Amélie.

—Oh, it's you! she said, even before grasping that David was calling her at home on a Saturday afternoon, in defiance of all their conventions.

— Amélie, don't you have anything to tell me? he asked in a sepulchral voice.

Taken aback, she stammered:

—No . . . perhaps . . . I'm so sorry about what happened. I hadn't planned lunch at our restaurant . . . Forgive me . . . Seeing you took me by surprise, and embarrassed me.

There was a silence. Amélie had nothing else to say, and since David didn't seem inclined to break this pause, she got angry with him. Wasn't it just like him, this heavy awkwardness! In his place, she'd feel hurt, keep a grudge perhaps, but after his apologies, she'd claim she understood, even at the risk of throwing it back in his face ten years hence. "After all, we can't spend the whole day on this nonsense," she thought, getting hot under the collar.

—David, what's the matter? What else d'you want me to say?

—You might begin by telling me with whom you were having lunch today? he hissed.

Amélie panicked.

—You wouldn't believe me if I did tell you.

—Then I'll be the one to tell. His name is Serge Munz. He's thirty-four, entered the Conservatoire in '79, after a stint at the rue Blanche drama school. He acted in three commercials, had two minor roles in soaps. He lives from one measly job to the next, mostly dubbings and postsynchronizations.

Stunned for a moment by this detailed report, Amélie kept silent. The worst had happened. She couldn't fall into the soup, she was already in it up to her neck. Then her curiosity returned. How had this inquiry been conducted, and to what end? Hardly the time to ask him to account for his research, she thought ironically . . .

—Now you're going to explain, David said threateningly.

Amélie quickly concocted her nervous response. "The head in the noose never speaks," she'd often remind herself.

She concluded early in life that admitting to a fib cast discredit upon the most straightforward declaration. David wouldn't believe her story of her encounter with her neighbor unless she stuck to the scenario of a family weekend. She'd lie a bit longer before serving up the truth. Taking a beat, she launched into her tale:

—Well, here's the story! This morning, Paul took the girls to the zoo. I didn't call you because I had no idea how long it would take. I was home alone . . .

—You must be joking. I'm not asking you for your morning timetable. You can't tell me you need hours of time to give me a call, he exploded.

No sooner had he completed this sentence than David felt sure Amélie was lying. He perceived how she had unrolled a screen of scrupulous precision in order to project her candid explanation. Of course she'd spent the morning with Serge Munz. Otherwise why insist on depicting herself as alone? Why else wouldn't she call him?

—Good Lord, let me finish! If I tell you all this, there's a reason! I never set eyes on Serge Munz before this morning, and I'm going to tell you how I met him.

—You're very clever, Amélie. I'm really curious to hear the rest of your story. So, how did you meet him? At the bakery, or the newsstand? Go on! I can tell I'm going to enjoy it.

The arm Amélie raised to emphasize her plea fell down. Certain now she wouldn't succeed, particularly in convincing David, she was ready to quit. However, her silence did nothing but inflame the scene David was making:

—Listen, David, this fellow is my neighbor. He lives right above me, and he flooded my living room when drawing a bath . . .

—Hats off! Well done! That's a lucky find, all right! And so, to celebrate your mutual mop action, you went out to lunch! Then, when I arrived, you chose to pass him for your husband rather than introduce him to me.

—Well, if that's how you're going to take it, Amélie said in a weary voice, if you don't believe me, it's your problem!

—My problem, he howled, don't you think it's also yours?

Then his attitude softened. Amélie was releasing her hold; he'd lose the match:

— Amélie, if you love me, if you ever loved me, listen. I was ready to accept anything coming from you. Jealous and vain as I am, I was willing to share you with your husband. You could have told me anything: that you met someone . . . no longer wanted me! I would have vanished from your life without a word, without trying to see you again. Rather die!

—But David, I swear . . . , Amélie mumbled, unwilling to admit to a fictitious affair.

—No, spare me! Haven't you taken me for enough of a ride?

This accusation opened the floodgates of Amélie's bad conscience. A brief review of her subterfuges, dodges, her reticence in regard to David, convinced her.

—Yes, you're right!

—Ah, you see! he clamored triumphantly, before savoring the bitterness of his perspicacity. It's not even hard to say! Sounds rather good: *"I've got to tell you, David, Serge Munz is my lover . . ."* Or: *"Look David, I found another lover . . ."*

—But . . . , Amélie ventured weakly, out of politeness.

—Do you prefer a solemn tone: *"David, I owe it to myself to tell you that Serge Munz is my lover . . ."* Come on, Amélie, some guts! I want to hear it from your lips! David's glibness gave him a high.

—All right, David, if this is what you want, Serge Munz is my lover.

She couldn't get over the ease with which she uttered this dreadful statement. David lashed her with his tongue:

—Is that all? Nothing to add?

—No, nothing.

—Then I believe we have nothing more to say to one another, David said in a choking voice.

He hung up.

*A*mélie was no longer comforted by her innocence, now that David's accusations had come to an end. Her scruples sank into silence. Suddenly she was disgusted with herself.

—Great! she mumbled. What a pathetic way to end an affair!

She could have told herself that this grotesque lie had spared him a cruel truth. Rubbish! She'd been afraid; afraid of telling him she no longer loved him; afraid of his reaction; afraid of suffering. She had taken refuge in imposture. David's jealousy was groundless, she couldn't reach it.

She was wondering what David was doing. Was he feeling remorse, a remnant of love? He must feel lost. Was he sad or angry? Was he trying to puzzle out the reasons for their quarrel, or getting drunk? Pain was lying in wait for him. It was his turn now to eat shit.

How ridiculous! she scolded herself. She was like a child at the movies, covering her eyes with her fingers, then spreading them open to find out what was happening. She'd just broken with David, yet was ready to call him to find out how he was, to comfort him.

It was over. The evening they'd met, she'd felt desire and concern, then her impulse had worn away, torn to shreds by the brambles growing all along love's path. All that was left was to draw a lesson from this, she mused, repressing a nostalgia for her erstwhile fervor. Why fall in love if falling out of love was inevitable?

The telephone rang.

David! she thought, taken aback. Was he considering making up with her, or did he wish to elicit additional details about her liaison with Serge Munz? Perhaps he simply wanted to insult her?

—Hello? she said, her voice full of apprehension.

—Serge Munz. Her neighbor announced himself in the tone of one resolved not to be timid.

—Ah, it's you!

Serge was piqued by Amélie's perceptible disappointment. The fact that he had leafed through his address book before calling her made no difference. His neighbor didn't have to know she was used as a last resort when his other conquests were busy elsewhere. Amélie's indifference eclipsed his own; she checkmated him. He inquired:

—Am I disturbing you?

His tone was quarrelsome; Amélie softened her answer.

—No, not in the least.

—Are you all right? he insisted, feigning worrying about her. Her stupefaction would be ungracious, were it to last any longer.

Serge's voice attracted Amélie's attention to David's silence. Her eyes were brimming with tears. Did she actually miss David, or was her self-indulgent pain brought on by Serge's solicitude?

—Not bad, she answered, resolved not to drown in self-pity.

—Your boyfriend, right? Things didn't work out.

—Yes, she sighed.

—You want me to drop by? Only one floor down for me . . .

—No, she protested weakly.

What would she do with him? She couldn't explain herself freely in his presence if David called back. All her reactions would be skewed. She had to be alone; even if David didn't call . . .

—Listen! Here's my suggestion, Serge insisted. I'll drop by in an hour; we'll go out for a drink somewhere. It'll take you mind off your troubles. All right?

—All right, she agreed, partly to get rid of him and leave the telephone line free—David might call any moment—and partly to hear Serge's warm voice dispelling her distress.

She paced through her apartment, beguiling her ennui by doing a bit of housework. When it became clear that David wouldn't call, she began to get angry. What was she hoping for? David's call? What for? She didn't have the slightest desire to get back with him. So?

Was she surprised he'd been taken in by her rudimentary lie, or hurt by the ease with which he accepted their separation? One might as well turn the page, she thought. The time had come to live serenely, without a courtly attendant.

The doorbell rang.

"Oh, merde! Serge Munz!" Amélie remembered, looking at her watch. "I'd forgotten him completely. And I haven't even changed . . . nor glanced in the mirror. I must look a fright!"